Advance Praise for

DONNER PARTIES

"Keith Cadieux's *Donner Parties and Other Anti-Social Gatherings* is always smart, occasionally heartbreaking, and just the right amount of over-the-top—it's everything I love about horror."
– **Nick Cutter, author of *The Troop* and *Little Heaven***

"*Donner Parties* is an intricate blend of stories and essays of the strange, macabre, meditative, experimental, the cosmic and weird—unsettling in the way it makes the mundane horrific, while exploring the nebulous boundaries of what is and isn't considered horror, along with chilling journeys that sweep across eerie Canadian landscapes."
– **Ai Jiang, Nebula and Bram Stoker award-winning author of *Linghun***

"Cadieux's complementary essays and stories in *Donner Parties and other Anti-Social Gatherings* are inextricable from each other, creating a sustained work of horror that is both conversational and discomfiting. A unique and exciting collection."
– **Naben Ruthnum, author of *Helpmeet***

"With stories that range from the quietly unsettling to the deeply and uncomfortably disturbing, Cadieux's masterfully written collection compels the reader to relish in the same obsession as its frame's author—to both seek out and interrogate what horrifies us."
– **Joanna Graham**

"*Donner Parties and Other Anti-Social Gatherings* tackles what we fear head-on, especially if what we fear isn't the most conventional. From the first story and throughout, *Donner Parties* places empathy at the centre of horror— where others look away in disgust or revulsion, Cadieux's characters peel back the curtain and take a closer look. This collection is a perfect read for those who scare themselves before someone (or something) else does."
– **Amy LeBlanc author of *Homebodies* and *Unlocking***

"These stories hook their teeth into you and burrow under your skin. Cadieux is a virtuoso of the creepy, the murky, the subterranean - these stories are as surprising and horrifying as fingers grabbing your toes from the depths of a midnight pool."
– **Suzette Mayr, author of the Giller Prize Winner *The Sleeping Car Porter***

"Grotesque in its intimacy, *Donner Parties* is a dismembered text haunted by its own author. Cadieux's writing offers a viscerally entangled exploration of the horrific self."
– **Erica McKeen, author of *Tear* and *Cicada Summer***

DONNER PARTIES

atbaypress.com

Canada Council   Conseil des arts
for the Arts   du Canada

We acknowledge the support of the
Canada Council for the Arts.

MANITOBA   CONSEIL DES ARTS
ARTS COUNCIL   DU MANITOBA

With the generous support of the
Manitoba Arts Council.

Keith Cadieux

DONNER PARTIES

and Other Anti-Social Gatherings

Winnipeg

For Mom and Dad, who let me be weird.

Acknowledgements

This book has been in the works for a long while and there have been many people along the way who have proven invaluable to its completion. Perhaps most materially (and financially) by grants from the Winnipeg Arts Council and the Manitoba Arts Council. I am beyond grateful to live in a place with access to these hugely important programs.

Early drafts of most of these stories benefited greatly from insights, suggestions, and encouragement from Seyward Goodhand, Joanna Graham, and Barbara Romanik. This book wouldn't be what it is without them.

To my friend Adam Petrash, for looking at early drafts, providing more encouragement, and an invaluable ear for all things writing, emotional, personal.

Many stories were also bettered by the mentorship of Jonathan Ball, a writer who keeps me on task and always seems to produce more work than I, even when we stick to the same schedule.

To Susie Moloney, for invaluable advice and suggestions. This would be a much different and weaker book without her.

To my family, for yet more encouragement and years of enduring my oddity and never making me feel as strange as I know I am.

And to Lindsey, above all, for everything.

Table of Contents

An Introduction by the Author

I wonder if most people remember what they were afraid of as a kid. I do. My parents didn't go out of their way to protect me from most scary things like books or movies, but at the same time I wasn't scared of predictable, conventional stuff. There doesn't seem to be a way to predict which events or images will leave permanent scars on children, so trying to protect them from fear usually doesn't work.

I was afraid of odd things. I was afraid of cutting the underside of my toes on the edge of the landing leading out the backdoor of the house I grew up in. For some reason that edge seemed especially sharp. We didn't go to church much but I was scared of being visited by a broken and bloodied Jesus, fresh from the crucifixion. I had a nightlight of Pluto, Mickey Mouse's dog, and many nights I lay awake with a terror that the glowing cartoon dog was growing bigger and more feral until it was big enough to fill the whole room, with a snarling and dripping snout, nosing at me hidden under the covers.

I was afraid of talking to people I didn't know. I didn't even like talking to people I did know. I still don't, really. I was afraid to be noticed by bullies or ghosts and so I worked to make myself invisible. I had a tendency to cover my face, with hoodies, scarves, under blankets. I even wondered if maybe I had been born with a caul, since having some barrier between my face and the world felt so comfortable. I was a little bit scared of just about everything and so I felt afraid almost all of the time. This was normal for me. A normal that I began to seek out.

By the time I was eight or nine I had a growing understanding of what specifically scared me and I went looking for more of it. I scoured the school library for books on ghosts—not stories but the *real* ghost books—and checked them out over and over. I remember one still, pages of photographs that had caught "REAL ghosts on film!!" There was a photo negative of a family packing up their station wagon for a road trip. Mother and kids were posed in front of the car, Grandmother already sitting straight-spined in the backseat, looking right at the camera. But she only appeared in the negative, not the finished photo. She had died the year before. Even if it was made up, the idea sent a shiver of dread through my body.

Another book had written accounts of ghost sightings and interactions accompanied by cartoonish illustrations. One story from the early 1900s mentioned a man staying alone in a big empty house. In the night he would wake up because of pressure on his chest and he saw a horrid ghostly face hovering above his own. When he made eye contact with the apparition, icy and invisible hands seized him by the throat and choked him nearly to death. In the illustration the ghost's face was blue, sticking out its tongue in a not-especially-menacing fashion, and blue disembodied hands floating in the air. Evidently the illustrator had a hard time conveying the invisible part. Despite this inherent goofiness, the story terrified me, and I would lie awake with my head fully under the covers, certain that there was a face floating just above me. As long as I stayed behind the mask of the blanket, maybe I would make it through the night. I asked my mother repeatedly if I had been born with a caul. She was always disgusted by the question and refused to answer.

But come morning, despite having spent the night nearly unable to breathe under the covers, I would wake up wanting more. I don't think I comprehended that what I liked was horror—I didn't seek it out in that kind of knowing way yet—but I chased the feeling of being scared. Even when I was so scared that it affected other parts of my life.

Well into my twenties I still couldn't fall asleep without the TV on. Even today, fighting through occasional insomnia, I'll pull the covers over my head and make a mental note to try and wake up before my wife so she doesn't notice. But despite all that—fear relieved—and still relieves, pressure in other areas. Without that release, I probably wouldn't have ever slept at all.

It could be argued that I was just anxious, maybe to the point of a disorder. I was always imagining the worst case scenario of any given situation. I didn't like to talk to people because my mind flooded with the worst possible thing the other person could say or do to me, which would sometimes happen anyway. I was a very small kid and got picked on. I would avoid with great effort even the briefest interactions, like talking to cashiers or other kids' parents. I was awkward, as well as puny. Horror provided a kind of outlet for those

3

feelings of awkwardness and especially for the anger at being bullied.

There is usually some kind of comeuppance in horror. The worst behaved characters meet a grisly end. Hannibal Lecter only eats the rude. Ghosts ultimately get their murderers (or their descendants). More importantly to the anxious little boy I once was, what sets horror apart is its willingness to fully embrace the worst-case scenario. Every horror story is essentially the worst possible way that scenario could play out. For someone normally brushed off with, "Oh you're just being silly," horror provides a rebuttal. Sometimes, the worst thing is *exactly* what happens. You'd best be prepared. Horror whispers back, "See! I was right. That's why I run up the stairs at full speed after flicking the lights off." And usually, it's the awkward and overcautious characters who make it through to the end.

Over time, my taste in horror became more refined. Not that the horror I sought out was better in quality but only that I better understood the types of horror that had a stronger effect on me. Vampires and werewolves have lost whatever hold they may have had. There are too many zombies. I find serial killers oddly fascinating though not viscerally scary. Demographically speaking, I'm much more likely to *be* a serial killer rather than the victim of one. I prefer the slow build to the shiny splash of gore. I still have a special affinity, if not continued dread, for ghosts, which is the sub-genre that is the most concerned with comeuppance and righting past wrongs.

There are, to be fair, real problems and logistical issues with horror as a genre, just as there are with any other. Despite being the best descriptor available, the word "horror" doesn't reveal much about genre or categorization. It describes a mood, an effect, rather than any details of format or convention and there are a number of expected conventions and tropes. At the same time, horror is welcoming of virtually anything which elicits that desired effect. Just like any other literary genre, there are shining examples as well as abysmally bad ones.

I mentioned earlier those examples of imprinting moments from my childhood and early exposure to horror to illustrate a counterpoint to what I think is a false assumption about horror fans and especially creators and artists who work in the genre: *that we are not in it for the scares.* That instead we are so desensitized to everything horrific that we simply enjoy a voyeuristic cruelty, basking in depraved glee at stories and images from which normal, well-adjusted people would turn away in disgust. This simply isn't true.

I only have my personal experience to draw on, I suppose, but I am keenly susceptible to all of horror's many tricks. I turn on all the lights when I'm alone in a room, check all the corners and cupboards and cabinets and closets before going to sleep. I jump at scary movies. I also deeply enjoy that feeling and keep returning to it.

What might be perceived as desensitization I would argue is familiarity. And yes, there is a distinction. As with any creative form, it becomes harder to enjoy something if it's derivative, too predictable, or too close to something we've seen before. When horror leans on the same tired tropes over and over (oh, he goes mad at the end of the journal? Surprise! The ghost is really the spirit of the spurned aunt they made live in the attic? I never could have guessed!) the result is frustration, disappointment, rather than fear. If a work of horror fails to get a reaction for a horror fan, it's probably just not all that good and not some faulty emotion on the part of the audience.

This familiarity does not mean that horror fans do not experience the emotions that horror is meant to evoke. The power in horror lies in the reader's sensitivity. The whole point is to be horrified by the content, to be unsettled by it. Horror is an art form centered on empathy, not depravity. The genre has always gotten a raw deal, always been derided. Even during the peak moment of horror as a popular form of entertainment—the 70s and 80s horror boom—it was never regarded as good art but rather as acceptable trash. A guilty pleasure. I'd like to say that the tide is turning but there is still resistance.

There continues today an avoidance of the bare term "horror" and prominent works in the genre are often stamped with new terms, coined just for them, to keep them unsullied and away from the reek of the dreaded H word: post-horror, art-horror, elevated-horror, psychological thriller, dark fantastic. Ultimately these allude to the same thing and the coded signifier remains unchanged. These are all Horror, if you were to ask me.

At some point, seeking horror out simply wasn't enough. It no longer scratched that itch, at least not on its own. So I began writing it myself. It wasn't a conscious choice, more of a compulsion which I think is true of any artist. The darker thoughts in my head were no longer fully exorcised by books or movies or outside sources, though I continued to devour and love them as I still do. To get my head clear and closer to that of a normal and well-adjusted person, the dark parts had to come out on their own, out onto the page. So here we are.

Despite a continuing urge in critical and popular circles to shy away from the genre as a legitimate or—God forbid—important art form, horror has always been present and has always helped to move literature along to new heights. One of the earliest novels written in English, Matthew Lewis' *The Monk*, is an out-and-out horror story. Two pillars of the western canon, *Dracula* and *Frankenstein*, could not be better examples of horror literature but I've never seen them identified as such on high school and university syllabi. *Beloved* by Toni Morrison is a blend of real-world and supernatural horrors, complete with a haunted house and a ghost. The Bible, all religious texts really, are teeming with the horrific. Yet there is still this squeamishness around horror. Artists who work in the genre know the following social reaction well, in polite conversation with "normal," "well-adjusted" people, say at a work party or a holiday event hosted by in-laws:

"What kind of stuff do you write?"

"Horror."

"Oh." Raised eyebrow, a pinched-lip smile, maybe a nervous chuckle. "Good for you. I can't stand that stuff."

This leads me then into a pretty obvious question: Why? Given all this negativity, why horror? First of all, why the hell not? Any argument against horror tends to skew overly simplistic, failing to completely consider the genre's conventions, its questions, its possibilities. There isn't really a good argument against horror since it all boils down to accepting the given premise that horror itself is fundamentally bad and should be avoided. The genre is not so easily pigeon-holed.

Horror is usually assumed to be a moral negative but this is flawed reasoning. Just as philosophical pessimism argues against the given and often default conclusion that life itself is inherently good—despite any and all suffering or individual experience—and thus should be preserved at all costs, so too does horror literature begin by examining a version of the world where all is *not* well. The opening agreement between the work and the audience in horror is that things are not as they should be. Bad things are happening. In reality, it is this kind of world where we all must live our lives.

7

The classic horror story, the tale of a monstrous evil whether it be an entity or a mode of thought, is often a surprisingly conservative affair, making the ultra-conservative stance opposed to horror all the more flummoxing. The classic setup begins with an idyllic normal, the happiness inherent in a good, usually Christian, heterosexual life. For example, the coming promise of a proper marriage as Jonathan Harker ventures into the scary wilderness of *not*-England to make his fortune. Love letters fly between himself and his creamy-skinned betrothed Mina, who waits ever patiently for her love to return. Until the beautiful idyll is shattered by the arrival of the monstrous Dracula, a creature of horrid and yet alluring appearance who comes from "over-there" and consumes anyone who is not striving hard enough for the good Christian family life that Jonathan and Mina are pursuing. Eventually the purity of our heroes is tested, upheld, and the monster is vanquished, rewarding the pure of heart with a return to the status quo. The monster—the aberration—must be destroyed so that we may return to the established normal which is always assumed to be inherently, even divinely, *good*.

Modern horror, thankfully, no longer seeks a return to the status quo. There are counter examples of course but in most modern horror, the status quo *is* the monster. The genre has been gloriously taken up by the marginalized voices of society, embraced by those who are not content to sit back on the given premise that life as it is now is inherently good. For them, for most of us, all is *not* well. And horror is the lens through which we may convince some of you holdouts of how the world actually functions.

What I have collected here I do not present to you as shining examples of horror as it should be. I don't believe these stories I've written and included here are the best that the

8

genre has to offer. I haven't mastered anything. I mean, I like them. But I include them here not as examples of success (material rewards thus far would suggest that they are not entirely successful) but rather as examples of how I understand horror to work.

These are the eventual result of my never-ending compulsion to get such thoughts out of my head. Even so, I do hope they offer some enjoyment. If you're so inclined, consider the other essays at each section break. I'll dive a little deeper into the things that are not well and the horror lens that might make those problems clearer. If you've read this far, I think you might be ready to see through the dark lens, if only for a while. To see the darker parts of the world around us reflected back and to ponder over those ideas.

Not voyeuristically. Not cynically. But empathetically. With eyes open. Come. Let's be pessimists together.

HOLDING HANDS

I think she was up to something," said the neighbour, Mrs. Kingsbury. The old woman sank deeper into her armchair and took a noisy sip from her mug. "It must have been three buses at least to get all the way here from the North End." Even from behind the refrigerator door Spencer could hear the whole conversation between the lady from two houses down and his mother. "Just to take that little boy to the outdoor pool over here," she went on. She even shook her head. "I don't believe any of that. And then she left him there all alone."

"What plan could she have then, to leave him here?" That was Spencer's mother.

"I'm not saying it was smart." Mrs. Kingsbury slurped from her cup. "Their neighbourhoods have their own pools she could have gone to."

Spencer's ears blushed and felt warm, hearing something he knew he wasn't supposed to. Dana was waiting for him downstairs. Getting bored. He rested his hand on two pop cans.

"Don't be naïve, now." Mrs. Kingsbury lifted the newspaper off the coffee table and dropped it down closer to Spencer's mother. "You look in there and read what it says about that neighbourhood they lived in." His mother sighed and swallowed a little of her tea. "That sort of woman wouldn't have come all the way here for that boy. She had her own little scheme and we shouldn't be wasting our time on that sort."

Spencer still pretended to look in the fridge, waiting for the next horrible thing the woman might say.

"Spencer Miles, do not just stand there with the fridge door open," she said.

"Sorry," he said. It was a reflex.

"Bring the kettle in here and refill the pot. It should still be hot."

Spencer closed the fridge and took the kettle into the living room. "I do feel bad for the boy," Mrs. Kingsbury said.

"And take the paper away. It can go in the recycling," said his mother.

Spencer brought the kettle and the paper back into the kitchen. The newspaper had been opened and scattered and refolded. He looked through the out-of-order pages, skipping over the "Autos" section, "Business." The arts section had a full page book review, "Experimental True Crime Puzzles Reviewer." Normally Spencer liked reading the book reviews but today he rifled through pages until he found the "Local" section.

MOTHER OF BOY ABANDONED AT
PUBLIC POOL STILL MISSING

After nearly two weeks of searching, police have reached out to the public for help in locating a local woman last seen at an outdoor public pool. The woman was reported missing by a friend of the family after her son found his way home alone. The identity of the woman is being withheld in order to protect the identity of the child.

The boy claimed to authorities that he asked several staff at the pool for help when he couldn't find his mother but was repeatedly dismissed. When the pool closed, he returned home by bus and visited the family friend for help, who then called police.

Spencer paused over the words a moment and then tossed the paper into the recycling bin. He opened the fridge once more, grabbed the two cans, and rushed downstairs.

He put the cans down on the end table and sat next to Dana on the loveseat. She was clicking through the channels too quickly for him to discern anything in particular. Once he was settled, she pushed a frigid foot under his thigh and pulled the little afghan up to her chin. They'd been side by side, close enough for him to put his arm around her, before she'd asked for a drink. Now she had her back against the far armrest, her legs folded up between them. He settled for placing a hand on her knee.

"What do you want to do now?" he asked and opened his can with one hand.

She clicked through more channels without turning to look at him. "There's an outdoor pool near here, right?"

13

He nodded.

"Let's go swimming later. After it gets dark."

"It'll be closed by then," he said.

"Right." Dana sat up, withdrawing her foot. She reached for her drink, knocking his hand away. "That's the point. That'll make it exciting. We'd be the only ones there."

"What if it's closed for the season already? Summer's basically over. It might even be drained."

"We can figure it out when we get there." She sat cross-legged now.

"What about bathing suits?"

"Can't you just let something be fun." She turned, put her feet on the carpet. She took a quick sip from her pop. "This is too cold," she complained, setting it on the floor.

Spencer's house sat on a quiet little bay. Once it was dark, he and Dana headed outside. As they reached the door, he asked her to wait a second and then rushed upstairs to put swimming trunks on under his jeans without her knowing. He left his phone on his dresser to make sure he couldn't get it wet.

They held hands while they walked, even though his quickly got sweaty. The streetlights were on but the trees along the front boulevards kept most of the neighbourhood dark and sheltered. Dana insisted they walk in the middle of the road, their clasped hands dangling over the line of black tar that served as a lane divider. She had a wide gait and took long, elegant steps—so far apart that Spencer had a hard time keeping up. He wasn't short but she was a little taller than him and he couldn't match her stride. He looked at the road while they walked, watching their shadows elongate as they moved out of the reach of one streetlight, then shrinking as they came under the sweep of the next one. There were no cars, no one who needed them off the road. Still, walking in the middle made Spencer feel exposed. As though he were someplace he wasn't allowed.

"The water's probably pretty cold," he said as they rounded the corner off his bay and onto the main road. There was a sidewalk there and he tried to tug over towards it but Dana pulled his hand back. Her pace was still quick. "Too cold to swim, maybe."

"It was over thirty today," she said. She pulled on him again as they crossed the four lanes of the street against the light. "Think positive, Spenny."

He sighed. His calves were getting sore from syncopating his steps. "Around this corner," he said, pointing, trying to keep his voice level so he didn't sound out of breath. He caught little wisps of chlorine in the air. "Can you smell the water?"

Dana smiled and turned away, walking even faster, letting her cool hand slip out of his sweaty one.

He liked holding hands with her. The undersides of her fingers were smooth and delicate and always cool. Her feet were cold all the time, too. He liked when she jammed each foot alternately under his legs when they sat on the couch. Or when she slipped her hands under his shirt for warmth. The few times they had held hands, it was when he was enjoying it most that she pulled hers away. Without her yanking on him, though, he was able to walk comfortably. He ambled his way over to the sidewalk.

"Hurry up, Spenny," she said, looking back at him. He was quite a few paces behind. "I won't wait." She smiled but wasn't joking. She made a beeline up the short driveway, barely pausing at the five-foot fence. The swinging gate was padlocked shut. A sign showed it had been closed for the season yesterday but there was still water in the pool.

Dana was already most of the way over. The chain-link rattled noisily as she climbed. Everyone in the neighbourhood must have been able to hear this ill-advised, late-night pool break-in.

"Can't you be quiet?" he hissed before catching himself.

"What's your problem?" She hopped to the ground on the other side and glared through the fence at him. He shouldn't have said anything. She spun around and kicked off her shoes. "Why'd you even come then, Spenny?" He hated when she called him that. Almost enough to tell her so. He hated when everyone at school called him that, which they always did, because he hated it. But soon the summer would be over and she'd go right back to not calling him anything.

"You're not even going to come in?" she asked.

"No, I am. Sorry. I want to."

"Then do it. Not waiting, remember." She turned around, pulled her hoodie up over her shoulders and took down her yoga pants in one smooth motion. She was left in her underwear and a plain t-shirt.

Spencer stared. She had just taken her clothes off in front of him.

"I thought that would get your attention," she said.

"Right. Coming," Spencer said. He grabbed the fence and climbed carefully, keeping quiet. He struggled to get the toe-end of his flip-flops to fit in the spaces of the chain-link. It hurt his feet. He paused at the top, looking around at the houses, wondering how many disapproving neighbours were watching from darkened windows. There were two streetlights at either end of the pool, pointed over the water.

Dana hit the water with a splash. He jumped at the sound and the chain-link rattled. The lights seemed to grow brighter and tilt towards him like prison spotlights as he hopped over the wall. He looked hurriedly from house to house, sure to see bedroom windows lit up, porch lights flicking on, angry neighbours bursting through front doors, barking dogs and screaming babies woken from peaceful slumbers, the whole neighbourhood focused on, and outraged by, Spencer Miles's wrongdoing.

But there was nothing. Just the gentle sound of lapping water. The thud of his pulse. No one had heard anything.

There was a spray of air as Dana resurfaced. "It's not cold at all," she spat, then wiped her face. Spencer dropped to the ground. He took off his sweater and jeans, straightened the legs of the swim trunks he'd worn underneath. She was singing to herself, doo-doo-dooing the chorus to some song he knew but didn't like. She did that a lot. He wanted to think of it as a cute little habit of hers, an endearing and enjoyable quality. But it was annoying. He sat on the edge of the pool, legs dangling in the water, then lowered himself in.

He closed his eyes and dunked his head. He came back up with water running down the back of his neck and shoulders, over his face, a little streaming past his lips and even over his tongue. It tasted off. Something other than chlorine. He slicked his wet hair back and wiped his mouth, then let himself drift farther into the pool.

Dana dove under the surface again, slinking her way over to him. With the streetlights it was bright enough to see around but hard to make out the shape of anything under the water. There was no hope of seeing down to the bottom in the murk.

She came up for air a few inches from him, spraying water as she exhaled. Spencer didn't turn away, tried not to even blink with her face so close. She looked straight into his eyes, wrapped her arms around his neck, her fingers tangling in his hair. For a moment, there was just the faint sound of dripping water. Then she kissed him.

His wet skin cooled quickly in the night air but under the water's surface it was warm. Comforting. They both tread

17

water and her smooth legs touched and slid against his. She ground her body against him. He could feel her nipples through her wet shirt. He was hard. The water was calm, only small ripples radiating around them, keeping secret everything underneath. Dana scanned his face, locking eyes as she thrust against him. Then she stopped.

"Let's go down the water slide," she said. Spencer didn't respond, gently keeping his hands on her body. He didn't think breaking the kiss would mean they were done but evidently it was enough time for Dana to jump to a totally different thought.

She'd already untangled from him and was most of the way out of the pool. She headed toward the far edge where the slide perched over the water. She waved for him to come with her but he was embarrassed to get out of the pool just then.

"The water slide is so fun, Spenny."

"You've never gone down this one," he mumbled, remembering not to let her hear him this time. Her wet feet made slapping noises as she ran.

"Watch me go down," she said. The metal ladder reverberated at each of her steps. Once she reached the top and sat down, her wet skin squeaked against the dry plastic. "You're watching, right?" For a second, just a second, Spencer thought she seemed obnoxiously young.

He started to turn and face her but she didn't wait for him. The noise of her skin on the plastic grew louder and she shrieked on the way down. Her voice cut off as soon as she smacked the water. The splash hit Spencer in the face. He rubbed his stinging eyes and spat out what had gotten in his mouth. The taste was worse now. "Do you find the water tastes funny?" he asked. He spat and wiped his lips again, did this two more times before realizing his dripping hands were bringing more water to his mouth. The liquid seemed silty, filled with particles that blocked the light. It must be because it was dark out.

"Stop looking for things to complain about," she said. Her face shifted into a grin. "Okay, you go down the slide now."

"That's not really my thing," he tried as a dodge.

"What about me," she asked. "Am I more your thing?" Before he could answer, she was on top of him. She put her arms around his shoulders and stood on his thighs, pushing him under. When they were a few feet down she let go and swam off. She tugged at his hand, urging him to chase her.

Spencer normally liked to keep his eyes open while swimming but the streetlights didn't cut through the underwater gloom and he could hardly see anything. He caught sight of Dana's feet kicking away but soon lost her altogether. It was like swimming in lakes; silt and clay and sand kicked up from the bottom, fogging everything around. Though of course a cement pool couldn't be filled with silt. A much younger Spencer loved to plunge as deep as he could with eyes held wide, on the lookout for deep water creatures and other sunken terrors. Searching hopefully, but also afraid that he might actually see something. He found himself doing this now but the dirty pool water hurt his eyes. It was getting cloudier. And he was too old for such things, scanning a pool for monsters.

Eyes shut tight, he dove deeper and made wide, blind sweeps with his arms. Feeling around for Dana was more effective than looking. He figured he must be near the bottom and twisted over, groping with his feet for the solid contact of cement but not feeling it. With another sweep of his arms, he managed to grab hold of the tips of cold fingers. The smoothness he so enjoyed in Dana's hands was gone, these fingers pruney and rough as they slipped away from him. He swam upward for air instead of reaching out for her hand again. He wiped the stinging, foul-tasting water off his face. Dana had already resurfaced and looked to have gotten bored waiting for him.

"Are you going to go down the slide or should we just head back?" Maybe she was upset that he hadn't chased her properly. He didn't want her to climb out of the pool in a huff, ending their near-skinny dip.

"Sorry," he said, climbing out of the pool. "I'm going right now." He took small, careful steps up the ladder of the slide, water dripping off his shorts and pattering on the pavement.

He was near the top when he felt something stuck to his leg. He crossed his foot around the back of the opposite knee, trying to wipe it off. He looked down to see strands of long black hair curled around his ankle. Gross. He shook his leg hard, trying to get it off. To no avail.

"What's the hold up?"

Dana's hair was not that dark. Spencer pinched and pulled the strands off but they stuck to his fingers. He shook his wrist, which worked just as well as shaking his leg, and scraped his hand against the top rung of the ladder to get the hair off of him. He shuddered and took a deep breath.

At the top, he swung his legs forward and sat. The breeze turned his skin to goosebumps. He closed his eyes. The smell of chlorine crisped the air for a second, but underneath it he could still detect the funk of the water.

"Oh my god, Spenny," Dana said from the water. "Come on."

The plastic didn't squeak when he went down. The skin of his back felt hot from the friction. He held his breath and shut his eyes tight just before hitting the water. He sank fast. He was ready for the bottom.

He landed hard on top of something.

Air burst from his mouth, the wind knocked out of him. He flipped himself right side up and felt around in frantic sweeps. He tried to ignore the growing cramps in his sides. His arms rushing through the water muffled other noises. He thought he heard screaming. It was hard to tell where it was coming from.

He opened his eyes, water stinging. In front of him was the shape of a girl. He pushed forward. Closer. Saw huge, stuck-open eyes. Mouth gaping, lips pulled away from teeth. As though shrieking and sucking down air at the same time. He could still hear the screaming but it wasn't coming from her.

This woman was dead.

He rushed upward through the water, spluttered to the surface. He shouted. The screaming pierced into his ears. Even louder now. His momentum pulled the body up with him. He tried to get away, pushed at the shoulders, the crown of the head. It just came closer. Arms and hands floated on the water, pruned skin stretched over bony fingers, clawing gently. He tried not to look at its face.

He managed to grab the edge of the pool, pulling himself out of the water even as the corpse clung to him. As he rose, it slid down the front of his body. Its nose and the edges of its teeth scraped along his chest and stomach. He retched. Tasted bile. He kicked the body off of him and it drifted face down as he pulled himself onto solid ground.

Dana crouched in the corner of the fence, shrieking with every breath. Spencer ran, picked her up by the elbows. She'd pushed into the fence so hard it left a checkered pattern all down her side. He shushed her and repeated her name over and over until her lungs were too dry and too empty to make a sound.

"Go back to my house and call for help." He tightened his grip as he fought an urge to look back at the pool. It was clear from her face that she didn't understand. He tried to slow his thoughts. One of them needed to call for help. He'd left his phone at home. He didn't know if she had hers. And one of them had to wait for help to come.

"Go to my house," he started over. "Your stuff is there. Just go to my house and call for help."

She tried to pull free, about to start screaming again.

"You don't have to come back," he said.

He helped her over the fence and watched her sprint down the street. When she got to the turn that would take her to Spencer's bay, she went straight. Before long she was well out of sight.

He saw the neighbourhood wake up around him. House to house, first upstairs windows brightened, then a living room or kitchen. Porch lights coming on fast. A dog barked and was promptly shushed. No one moved beyond the safety of their front steps.

"I need an ambulance," Spencer yelled.

He was unsteady with no one to hold onto. He dripped with cold. His hands shook. His muscles ticked above his knees, like his legs were about to crumble. Moving around helped. He paced. Needed to do more. It was either do something or look at what was in the pool.

He gathered up his and Dana's clothes. Folded everything neatly. One piece at a time. He made a little pile next to the fence where she had climbed over.

There wasn't anything else to do. He tried standing quiet for a moment but the tics came back.

He looked at the water.

The body had floated out toward the centre but was still within reach. His pulse was loud in his ears, his stomach roiling. He should pull the body to the edge. Shouldn't leave her to drift out where she would need to be recovered with a net.

Or some kind of hook. He crouched at the edge of the pool but his hand barely reached the surface.

He lay flat on his stomach and inched himself out over the water. He grabbed hold of her ankle. Pulled her close. He shifted onto his knees and took her forearm in one hand. He put the other under her chest and lifted her by the side. Her skin was slick and spongy. He turned her face up.

He tried to imagine what she'd looked like without the bloated, purplish skin. Without the stuck-scream of her mouth. Eyes that weren't stretched wide and milky with chlorine, without the veiny mass of burst blood vessels under the eyebrows. Her hair was a deep black that reflected the light.

He sat on the edge of the pool, careful to cross his legs so they didn't dangle in the water. Still holding her forearm, he felt a lilting tug. Even now something tried to bring her farther away, out of anyone's grasp. He listened and hoped for the sound of sirens. He was going to have to explain what he was doing here, where he shouldn't be. He could almost hear Mrs. Kingsbury slurping her coffee, shaking her head. His ears blushed and grew warm at the thought. But the woman in the pool felt so cold. And he didn't have to leave her here alone.

He didn't have to leave her at all. He could keep her close, keep her from drifting out where no one wanted to reach. He didn't need to discard her as others had. No one had even looked. And not sure what else to do, and feeling like a lost little boy, he put his hand inside of hers.

DONNER PARTIES

Lewis Keseberg is the name he's used to rent out the decrepit basement of the rooming house. He leaves an envelope of cash in the mailbox every month, has seen the landlord only once, and either there are no other tenants or they never leave the place.

To call it an apartment would be too generous—there are two rooms with poured concrete for walls and a floor. Squat, splintered windows sit at eye level, ground level on the outside, and he hears every car that passes by, though there aren't many of those. The tires going past intermingle with other sounds: a rattling refrigerator, a steady sewer-filling drip. The floor is slick with water, which runs into a small metal drain.

He wears a sleeveless white undershirt, worn khaki trousers and plain white socks. Water squelches out of the fabric and between his toes with each step, but he prefers this to the feel of the cement on his bare feet. He sports a full beard, a spade, that reaches to his chest. The long whiskers drip down onto the front of his wet shirt and pants.

His fingertips are pruned and slippery with wet. Loosely, by the handle, he grips a gallon jug filled with water. He paces and stops at the edge of the drain, plants his feet, takes a few deep breaths, and brings the jug to his lips. He tilts his head back and drinks, making loud pulsing sounds as he forces down water. His palate notes hints of copper. His esophagus stings with cold before going numb. His stomach shrieks and distends as it's forced into holding so much fluid. He tilts too far and it spills out the sides of his mouth. He loses his focus, coughs, splutters, and has to pull the jug away. There are still a few cups of water left in the jug.

He rests his hands on his sore belly, tries to catch his breath but belches instead. The square, stone room reverberates, just for a second, then the sound of the burp is overtaken by a rush of water as he vomits all that he has drunk onto the floor. He bends forward at the waist, pushes hard on his middle, squeezing out as much as he can, like spritzing juice from a lemon.

He dumps out the little bit left in the jug. He straightens up and moves over to the side of the room where there is a sink with no counter. He refills the jug, to the very top.

Warmed up now, he needs fewer breaths to fill his lungs and brings the container back up to his mouth to drink. And drink. This time he drains the gallon without a hiccup. He doesn't think he's spilled any, but he is too soaked to be sure. He straddles the drain, presses hard and low on his belly, and forces everything out again. He makes a fist around his beard, wrings out the excess. His belly is sore and cold. Satisfied.

This is part of his training. Gorging on water stretches the stomach. A folding dinette table is set up against the wall opposite the sink. The legs wobble on the sloping floor. The tabletop is covered with medical and anatomical textbooks, all thick, heavy hard covers. Some are piled neatly, others opened to specific pages and lain atop each other. He is always careful not to get them wet but the pages are wavy and moist. The glossy finish of the coloured paper is dulled in straight lines where he has run a damp fingertip along the words, memorizing all the terms and structures and layouts of the stomach, its surrounding muscles, the placement of nearby organs, the distribution of nerve endings, where fat tends to roll over, how deep the stomach lining, the careful coiling of the intestines. He knows this information by heart but reading the words over again is part of the training as well. The ritual.

There is one book that doesn't fit with the others. A thin paperback, popular history rather than a textbook. He reads and rereads familiar words, savoring a favourite texture: *When they asked him why he had not eaten the ox legs, he replied, 'They have not as good a flavour.'* He closes this book first and sets it at one end of the table. He closes the others one by one and sets them in a neat stack atop a cinder block in the corner. The table now cleared, he steps over to the noisy fridge, the bone-metal rattle louder with the door open, and takes out a glass punch bowl filled with fresh stewing beef. He sets the bowl on the dinette table and pulls over a kitchen chair from against the far wall. He peels back the plastic wrap and eats the small cubes of cold meat. Eating, of course, is part of the training as well.

The pieces are slippery and slide easily down the throat, thanks to a recipe of his own—sugar, corn starch, a touch of water—that makes the liquid viscous and slick, though admittedly it doesn't do much for the flavour. With pinched fingers, he lifts out and eats each morsel one at a time without chewing. Chewing slows everything down and the whole point is to consume as much as quickly as possible. He won't eat again for three days, not until the party. He will need to be hungry.

He stands, rinses the bowl, and leaves it in the sink. He wipes his mouth and face with a handful of tap water. At the other end of the basement is the empty bedroom. A separate outfit hangs neatly from wooden hangers over the doorknob, expensive shoes set atop an empty cardboard box, so as to be off the ground. He undresses, lays the wet shirt and pants flat on the cement floor to dry, tosses the balled, wet socks in the corner, and puts on the good, clean clothes. He turns out the lights, the raspy breath of the fridge still louder than the elegant clack of his footsteps. He will lay low, try not to be seen until it's time. He has to duck to step into the hall. He locks the door behind him, the sound of the key against the tumblers like cracking soup bones.

After three days, the night is dry and cold, but he enjoys the walk. The smells are crisp, his steps slow. Sunrise is still a few hours away. In one hand he swings a metal lunchbox, the kind he imagines construction workers eat from, up high on the girders. He smells the greasy, salty smoke of food vendors and his stomach growls.

He walks deep into downtown, crosses through an outdoor parking lot. He kicks a walnut-sized rock ahead of him for a few strides. The skip of the stone and his footsteps are the only sounds. His hands are cold and he puts one in his pocket, the other still holding the lunchbox, walks with his head high against the chilled breeze.

He walks half-a-dozen more blocks and stops in front of a long and low-roofed brick building. There is a FOR SALE sign in the window. No phone number is written on it. The power lines overhead buzz, as though coursing with honeybees.

Just in front of this one building it seems darker than the rest of the block. There is a lamppost right out front. He steps to it, glass crunching under his shoes, and looks up as he sits on the curb. He lets his gaze rise slowly like steam to the top of the post where the bulb is broken. He breathes deep, enjoying the scent of the air, the taste of anticipation. He relishes it, lets the air roll around his mouth, absorbing the feel. His stomach rumbles again.

He hears shambling feet, soles never lifted off the ground, and rusty shopping cart wheels. A shuffle and squeak. A greasy man makes his way up the road. Keseberg stays sitting, enjoying his quiet moment, but the man walks straight to him, hand outstretched. He has glassy eyes like washed and polished apples.

"Spare change?" the man says.

Keseberg admires the man's beard a moment, almost as long as his, except grimy and riddled with gray. He gets up to take a five-dollar bill from his pocket and hands it over. "Nice beard," he says. "How do you keep your food out of it?"

There is no answer and the man continues up the block, as though never interrupted. Keseberg stands in the same spot and turns to watch him go. The man reaches the end of the street, wheels around, and wanders back the way he has just come. The money now tucked away, hand outstretched again, eyes empty of recognition.

"Any change, sir?" the man says. It's Keseberg who doesn't respond this time. The man is unperturbed and moves to the far end of the block and turns onto the next street. Once he's out of sight, Keseberg slips into the old building. He's savoured enough.

Inside is a dark and unswept staircase leading down, though the lights in the room at the bottom are on. He takes the steps slowly and has to lean his head to one side to avoid hitting the angled ceiling. The lower level sprawls into a broad, open space. More than a hundred people, by rough estimate, mill and murmur about. They stand in small groups, huddle around support beams. Everyone whispers, a few chuckle nervously—a mixture of contained excitement and morbid curiosity simmering all around, bubbling at the edges.

As Keseberg steps deeper into the room, the crowd moves aside and fills in promptly behind him as he passes, like sauce parting thickly around a spoon. He meets the stares of those who turn to him, looking in their eyes for signs that they recognize him. He wonders how many have seen him eat before, how many know him by name.

"That's Lewis Keseberg," he hears crest over the thrum. He nudges people aside, looking for the source. He sees a youngish looking woman, her tattooed face close to the ear of a tall male companion who seems a little younger. She is pointing him out.

He approaches the pair swiftly, a smile liberally spread across his face to greet his fans. "I don't believe I've had the pleasure," he says, leaning forward. The woman looks sheepish and takes a step back and to the side, just enough to put her companion between herself and Keseberg. "Surely not first timers?" he says. The man deepens his furrowed brow and takes his own step back. Their fear sour like brine. Both ease their way backward, regaining their anonymity in the crowd. "No need for rudeness," Keseberg says, and shrugs.

He makes it to the front of the crowd, beyond which is a serving counter and past that a long-defunct kitchen with dusty and dulled stainless steel surfaces devoid now of appliances. As he takes in the full scope of the room, the layout of the open space with the kitchen behind, the neighborhood around the building, he realizes what this space was

30

normally used for: it's a soup kitchen. This makes him smile. Tables and chairs have been cleared away to make more standing room, which is already filled with bodies.

In front of the counter are three wheeled tables, each covered with a clean and pressed sheet. Under the covering, the familiar rising and falling shape signals to him that everything is in place and ready. The contest will be starting soon. The fluorescent bulbs overhead have been changed and there are tall halogen work lights at either end of the row of tables.

Two of the table stations are already claimed, their eaters nearby. Keseberg steps behind the one remaining, sets his lunchbox on a nearby tray, and leans back against the counter, hands in pockets. The metal tabletop in front of him is shaped like a deep, over-sized cookie sheet with a steep lip all around. Something straight out of a morgue. There is a digital console on the side with a weight read out: 176 lbs.

He nods to the eater next to him. "Hello, Armin," Keseberg says. Armin doesn't answer but this doesn't faze either of them. There is a woman hovering at the farthest station. She takes no notice of them.

A woman in a tie with round, frameless glasses approaches the row of slabs. She snaps on latex gloves and drapes a stethoscope across the back of her neck. She wants the eaters' attention. Keseberg takes his hands from his pockets and crosses his arms. "You know, the first time I competed, the event doctor actually wore scrubs and a mask." Armin shows a hint of a smile. "Glad to see it didn't turn into a trend," Keseberg says.

The event doctor nods to each eater in turn and pulls away the sheets. The whispering crowd catches its breath and holds it. A nude and lightly drugged man is laid on each slab. The doctor steps over to the one in front of Keseberg and presses two fingers under the corner of the jaw, below the ear. She pushes her glasses higher up on her nose and watches the man's chest rise and fall once before moving to the next. "Mister Keseberg, mister Miewes, are you ready?"

They both nod.

Keseberg eyes the woman at the far end. "Any word on her?"

Armin Miewes turns to him. "I haven't heard anything."

Keseberg squints against the light, still looking at the far station. "I'm not sure I like that," he says.

The doctor takes up a clipboard and a pen, raises one arm and holds her watch at eye level. The whole room stares at her. The silence grows frenzied, roiling. She drops her arm, the signal to begin, and everything boils over.

Keseberg opens his lunchbox and takes out two knives. He has refined his toolset to just these. He takes a long moment to look everything over, assess, even though the other two have already rushed to take their first few bites. He will not be pressed into making careless blunders. The sleeper before him is young, disheveled, but clean. His lips are cracked, angry sores in the crook of the elbow. Track marks.

He chooses his filet knife first, long and slender, and makes a very shallow cut across the stomach, left-to-right, through the navel. The sleeper's eyes flutter but don't open. The blood flows. That done, he changes to his slicing knife, with the granton edge, and starts in earnest at the shoulder. He carves a generous mouthful, a cube of stew meat, but doesn't lift it out right away. He gives the heart rate a chance to elevate, lets the juices swap around a little. Once it's coated over, he picks it up in his fingers, pops it in his mouth, and swallows without chewing. Warm and pleasing.

He feels prickles of sweat at his temples, in the small of his back. The lights are hot but give an excellent view around the whole room. He sees the crowd surge and bulge, though

32

it never comes too close to the tables. The doctor paces from station to station, keeping her distance as well, so as not to interfere. He moves slowly, takes in the moment, the sights and sounds. The smells and flavours. There is some commotion over at Armin's table, where the sleeper is awake and fighting.

They are never tied down, the sleepers. That would be cruel. Restraint and control are part of good technique and up to the eaters. The commotion works into the crowd, who roars with excitement and encouragement, but for whom is unclear. Keseberg looks down to see his own sleeper's eyes open and looking confusedly at the cut in his stomach. He begins to sit up and Keseberg helps roll him onto his side into a fetal position. The sleeper clutches at his belly, tries to press the cut closed.

"That's good thinking," Keseberg says, leaning over him close. He breaks good manners and speaks with his mouth full. "Don't let anything slip out." Though the cut isn't deep enough for that, just a distraction that helps maintain control. "It could be worse," he says as he swallows. "I hear there's a group that only eats the brain. Keep your hands on your belly."

Armin, on the other hand, has lost control. He is no longer eating at all, only struggling to hold the sleeper down. With every move the crowd reaction grows but after a moment Armin has no choice but to grab a heavy cleaver and bring it down with a roar.

"Back!" the event doctor says as she steps to the table. She places her fingers on the sleeper's neck and, when she doesn't feel anything, takes down the time on the clipboard. The doctor moves around to read the scale and notes the difference from the starting weight, which is just over two pounds. It's a poor showing. Armin swears under his breath and passes behind Keseberg on his way around the counter, leaving the competition area. "That's why you're not supposed to play with your food." He smirks around another bite.

The far station is suspiciously quiet, by contrast. That sleeper hasn't woken up at all. It happens from time to time, a miscalculation in the anesthetics. The doctor checks the pulse. "He's dead," she says and waves the eater away. The recorder comes around to check the scale. Her showing is well over six pounds. That may seem like a lot, more than is believable, but keep in mind the record for hot dogs is seventy-six, buns and all.

This leaves Keseberg the clear winner but he keeps eating. The doctor steps closer to his table, watching over the rim of her glasses. The sleeper is so preoccupied with the cut across his stomach that he can't offer much resistance, no matter what Keseberg is up to. The pen and clipboard are poised and ready. And Keseberg eats. He doesn't stop because he's full, or even because he's already won. Just puts his training to use.

The room is hushed, everyone curious to see how long it could possibly go on. A few at the front, if they strain their ears, can hear chewing, smacking lips. They start to whisper and Keseberg strains to hear them. He hears his name, hushed, as though his existence were a secret that they can't wait to share.

He almost feels the need to offer whispers of his own. To draw from the words, which he reads and rereads for his favorite texture, that describe the fourth team of rescuers expecting to find the last four survivors trapped in the Sierra Nevada mountains and finding instead three of them dead—partially eaten—and a wealth of ignored provisions including three ox legs. Only one man alive: Lewis Keseberg.

He sometimes passes people in the streets and wants

to tell them. He has heard strangers mention with a hush, *they're called Donner parties. My cousin's been to one. It's true, I swear.* They will forever relish whispering of him.

The doctor has her fingers on the sleeper's neck but she keeps quiet. There is still a faint pulse but it's fading. Keseberg slows but continues to eat. The crowd looks on, their excitement mostly drained. The lights begin to flicker. And Keseberg eats. And eats. The real shame is that eventually it will all come to an end. He will have to stop. But for the moment, at least, he sees no reason to.

A Difference of Tropes

My family doesn't like to watch movies with me. I tend to get frustrated when films are predictable and usually announce how I think the plot will play out. I'm usually right. After an incident that played out in just this way, my sister asked with considerable exasperation, "Why do you even watch movies, then?"

A few more imprinting horror moments from my childhood came from movies. My dad likes the *Star Trek* films and when I was ten, he wanted me to watch *The Wrath of Khan* with him. There's a scene where, as part of a brutal interrogation, a carnivorous earwig is placed in a man's ear and it proceeds to eat his brain, the man screaming until he dies. I was staring wide-eyed at the screen, muscles tensed to the point of discomfort, and my dad snuck up behind me and poked his finger in my ear. I stormed out. To this day I have not seen the rest of the film. I suppose movie watching issues run deep in the family.

Similar to seeking out more horror and more scares in books, I devoured movies, horror and otherwise scary ones in particular. Over time, just like any avid film viewer or anyone who has tried to craft a story, the similarities in stories, be they on film or the page, build up and eventually you can see how it is all put together. Once you realize where they are, you can see the strings, the stitches, the pieces.

I'm not alone in following horror from one medium to another. In general, fans of horror literature are mutual enjoyers of horror film. Because of this, there is a cross-pollination of ideas and concepts, a lateral genetic transference if you want to get fancy, that audiences of both media types understand. This allows for intertextuality between books and film, making horror almost a postmodern genre from the get-go, no matter which form is chosen.

Horror is constantly in conversation with itself and in order to keep readers and viewers scared and unsettled, it needs to change. Because of this, it is rewarding if the audience understands the tropes and conventions that are upended. This plays against expectations and creates a discomfort in not knowing. Humanity is most afraid of the unknown, after all.

For our purpose here I want to deal primarily with literary or written horror, which can be set aside as a distinct form in a number of ways. It is equally important to differentiate it further from horror film. As would be the case with any art form or genre, the tropes and conventions for each medium are different. For written versus filmed horror the reasons for the differences can be pared down to effectiveness: some of the most effective conventions for horror movies don't work on the page and likewise literary tropes often don't translate to a purely visual medium. Even so, horror books and films still manage a kind of interrelated conversation.

As a first example, consider the "final girl," which is probably the most recognizable and best understood trope of horror movies. This particular trope is also tied to one specific subgenre: the slasher.

The final girl premise is predicated on a reasonably hopeful outcome, essentially the conservative story structure I mentioned earlier. The climax requires the final girl to put down the monstrous threat and restore the order of the status quo. She is revealed as the foil to the monster by tests of her purity, usually by demonstrating she has superior values than the other victims who are dispatched one by one in the midst of committing immoral acts like drinking and fucking. By elimination, the purity of the final girl is brought into focus, bestowing on her the worthiness to combat the villain. With order restored, the final girl is rewarded with survival and a brief appearance in the sequel (the heroine from the original is usually dispatched almost immediately in the sequel, to make room for the new final girl).

There are counterexamples here and there, and many, many artists and critics long ago identified and examined this structure. Most modern slashers aim to surprise and so they avoid or twist the final girl narrative. At the same time, in order to subvert an expectation, it has to be clearly laid out. There must be a default from which a new work can differ so that it can question that trope and meaningfully upend it.

This formula doesn't work especially well spread out over a few hundred pages. I can't think of a strong literary example of the straight-on final girl stories to rival film examples like *Halloween* or *Friday the 13th* or *Nightmare on Elm Street* and on and on and on but there are quite a few novels written around the final girl. Readers are maybe more apt to enjoy that dismantling and contemplative structure but nevertheless it all relies on readers intimately understanding the basics of the final girl trope. The audience must be cross-pollinated for a literary work like this to succeed. Such a book must reach out past the boundaries of itself and draw in something from the world which exists outside the book. Pure magic.

Maybe I should share a trope that does work well in written horror, you say? Well, there is an element of the final girl trope—not exclusive to it but which commonly appears—that works well with virtually any work of suspense: the failure of authority or social infrastructure to confront, let alone comprehend, the threat. Be that threat monster or killer or what have you, there is often a tension as to whether or not the threat is real or imagined or exaggerated. In the final girl example, there are usually several instances wherein the protagonist tries to get help from an authority figure like a sheriff or, if you want to be really conservative, her husband or father, and is rebuffed. The authority assumes that the final girl is being hysterical, jumping at shadows until the threat does emerge with weapon in hand.

The main function of such figures seems to be an illustration of the danger in ignoring the veracity or reality of the threat. When these characters do come face to face with the slasher they almost never take in that information and adjust their behaviour. Instead, they resign themselves to their gruesome fate. It is better to die than acknowledge the existence of the monster and upend their own beliefs about the world around them.

Having characters or indeed an entire social infrastructure that is not equipped to accept the threat of the monster is an effective way to build tension and advance the plot. It works to isolate the protagonist and thus also the reader. Whoever does understand the threat is tasked with defeating or maybe simply surviving it. This is a core tension in most horror stories and especially those with first-person narrators. While not a hard and fast rule, a quick survey of horror literature—novels, short stories, novellas—would show the majority are written in the first-person. It's not required, it's just effective. This restricted perspective is much more difficult to achieve on film.

Particularly in a story with a monster, a first-person perspective creates a natural tension in the reader: is the narrator correct and the monster is real and it is coming for them? Are they mistaken, hallucinating, paranoid, suffering from some kind of mental illness or derangement? Are they outright lying? Should we, as the reader, align ourselves with the authority that doesn't believe in the monster?

The unreliable narrator is not specific to horror but it is one of the genre's most classic modes. Indeed, the unreliable narrator could be seen as a bridge between capital-L Literature and capital-H Horror, as there are plenty of examples of unreliable narrators in highbrow and canonized literature.

Where the unreliable narrator differentiates itself from the other horror tropes is that the tension largely occurs off the page. When it comes down to it, the reader only has what is written down, what is laid out in the book before them. An unreliable narrator raises the possibility of those words being deceptive. The reader must puzzle out the truth, using only the information in the text, which is essentially and fundamentally flawed. In some cases, it may even be dangerous for the reader to accept the version laid out by such a narrator. Or equally dangerous not to accept it because it is also possible for an unreliable narrator to tell the absolute truth. The boy who cried wolf did eventually see a wolf. The whole point is that the reader cannot know the truth, usually not until it's too late.

Allow me a quick aside: apologies if the language here has seemed overly sinister. I've a tendency to do that, one that hasn't gone unnoticed by family. One of my aunts once told me she was not at all surprised that I turned out to be a horror writer, and it was actually a relief because I had been such a creepy kid.

"One of the first times I came to visit after you were born," she said, "you were already four or five, and you just kept asking your parents why they had put the skin blanket over your face when you were a baby. And every morning, you'd mention it and then ask, 'Can I have it back?' I'd never seen such a look on your parents' faces," she said. But I digress.

There is another connecting thread between Literature and Horror which makes the two genres palatable to readers with tastes more aligned to one or the other of the two genres. I haven't found an agreed upon term for it, though the idea appears frequently, so I've settled on the "supernatural adjacent." There can be examples of this which lean more to sci-fi or fantasy or any other genre really but in the horror iteration, such stories involve a humanistic storytelling. They are very close to realist fiction but there is a trace, a faint colouring, of an element that exists outside the normal rules—the supernatural—that greatly affects the story's conflict. The key trademark of this trope is that the story reaches its climax without establishing the reality or non-existence of the supernatural element. The story will have a satisfying conclusion but this thread is left dangling.

A literary example would be Henry James's *The Turn of the Screw*. The ghosts of Miss Jessel and Peter Quint may very well be haunting the grounds of Bly Manor, and may even have possessed the bodies of the children, but this is never verified. All the reader can draw upon for evidence is the second-hand retelling of the contents of the governess's journal, in which the details of the haunting are said to be recorded. This example is also buried in layers of unreliable narration, making it an outstanding example of a whole range of horror tropes, many of which we won't even be able to get to in these short essays: a haunted house; retelling stories around a fire; a vulnerable lower class—worker, child, woman—at the mercy of the secrets and whims of a rich man; ghosts. Always the ghosts.

To bring us back to film, a modern and popular example of the supernatural adjacent would be the first season of the series *True Detective* written by Nic Pizzolatto and directed by Cary Fukunaga.

The basic plot is a murder mystery surrounding the deaths of sex workers and the disappearances of a number of children from poor families, but it is also tinged throughout with a supernatural literary reference: *The King in Yellow*. A short story collection by Robert W. Chambers and first published in 1895, *The King in Yellow* features a number of loosely connected stories that build a nebulous mythology around a dreaded figure. Known only as the titular King in Yellow, his kingdom is referenced in a forbidden play of the same title. Quite a few authors have added their own takes and twists to the mythos and there are whole anthologies dedicated to collecting these homages to Chambers's creation.

The play aspect does not factor into *True Detective* but the dark tone and tension of the show comes primarily from the unsettling nature of the clues and hints which point toward the possible existence in the real world of the figure mentioned in Chambers's short stories. Though the plot of the show does conclude with a realistic and entirely natural climax, the existence or non-existence of this supernatural figure is never settled. There remains the distinct possibility that in the Louisiana of *True Detective,* so similar to our real world, the Yellow King actually exists.

Where this trope works best is in a slow burn story. Ghost stories are usually slow burn affairs and when we're alone, in the dark and reading, it seems not at all a stretch of imagination to feel as though some figure, there and somehow not, is present with you. The tension builds and builds in small increments so that when the story's scares do arrive, they are often small but pull a huge response from the reader.

If the reality or nonexistence of a supernatural element is never satisfactorily revealed, (which is how the world of our reality actually works), then the scare is by necessity smaller and the rest of the piece needs to do that work of building tension. It need not always be scary, though that is usually the main goal of horror, but can work on a range of emotions like grief, loss, regret, sympathy, sadness. Delicate and subtle ghost stories are often more somber than shocking. A supernatural-adjacent element like a ghost or the Yellow King can be an effective tool to pull specific emotions to the forefront of the work. It is a nuance, something that is too often lacking in every genre. No need to beat us over the head with everything.

SIGNAL DECAY

"Hi Debra, it's Lori. I know you've all been waiting to hear from me for a long time now. Sorry. I don't have everything quite sorted out but there is something I need to show you. Please call me back. Bye."

Lori pushed the side button, putting the phone to sleep. She set it down on Tim's desk, next to the clutter and spread of papers. The tops of everything were dusty, the only clear spots in the shape of small finger swipes where Lori had briefly touched. She had meant to clear it all up, had even started to do it, but couldn't bring herself to finish. If the top was clean and free of clutter, it would be totally alien to what she was used to. It wouldn't be Tim's desk anymore.

She continued clicking through the hundreds of folders saved on his computer, and then scanning through the hundreds and hundreds of audio files tucked away in them. Over the last two weeks, she had made her way through quite a few; to her mind, she was making good progress. It was tiring work. Some of the files were only a few seconds, if even that. Some of them just micro snippets of one unique, painfully particular sound: a door closing; a door opening; a doorknob turning; a left footstep; a right footstep; a dog bark. Other files were hours long, hours of seemingly nothing. She had the hardest time with these. It was so tempting to just skip through them but she worried about missing what she was looking for. What a waste, if she were to just skip over it. She had a brief moment of triumph when she figured out how to open Tim's mixing software, rather than just using the music player, and one of the windows in that program showed a visual read out of the file: a level line that peaked upwards in sharp points when there was a sound that emerged out of the background. This made scanning the long files actually viable, as she just had to scroll along the line until something stood out and then she could play the file and listen to the specific sound, looking for him.

At first when she heard the sound of keys in the door, she assumed it was coming from the computer, part of the audio file. But then she heard Tim's mother say her name.

"Lori? Are you home?"

"Back here," she said. What time was it? She had only just left that message. Hadn't she? She clicked the program shut and turned the monitor off. She still felt it somehow improper to be seen going through Tim's things. Even though that's what she was supposed to have been doing for nearly a month now.

Lori stepped out of the tiny office into the apartment hallway to meet Debra, who was taking slow and careful steps into the kitchen, eyeing the pile of dishes and fast-food wrappers tossed on the counter, the empty wine boxes piled on the floor next to the blue bin. A bottle rarely lasted her a day, lately.

"I got your message," Debra said, pretending not to stare at the mess. "Should I put on some coffee for us?"

"Sure, that's fine," Lori said. She began gathering up some of the clutter and discovered that the garbage can was already full. She pulled the edges of the black plastic bag up, tried to cram more inside. Neither spoke while Debra rinsed the coffee pot and then filled the sink while the coffee maker began to sputter and hiss.

"Do you have any boxes for me to take, since I'm here?" Debra asked, drying her hands.

"Thanks for doing those," Lori said. "And no, no boxes yet."

"I'm about out of patience here, Lori. You won't let us come in and take anything but you're not doing any of the work. Not all of this stuff is for you. He has family who wants to remember him too. His sisters, his nephew, not to mention me and Gary." She folded the moist tea towel in half and draped it over the handle on the oven door. "And then there's the money side of it. None of us knew how badly in debt he was, the both of you were. We're trying not to leave you with all of it but if you don't want our help, then—"

"I know all this. You're not helping me but just dredging it up in front of my face. I can't just pack him up into boxes and be done with it. It doesn't work that way, not

47

after what he meant to me. This part isn't up to you. I knew him better than any of you." Her face was getting hot and red. Her throat felt blocked, a growth of pain trying so hard to claw its way up out of her and spew over the world she'd been left with.

Debra sighed. After one more breath she reached into the cupboard and took out two mugs, filled them with coffee. "If we sell his equipment, then we can make a real dent in the credit cards. The loans are more complicated but have more wiggle room," she said as she handed the mug to Lori.

"I've been working on that. I'm going through the computer, making sure that there isn't anything we should keep. Or anything useful, even. I might find someone who would buy all the gear among all his projects and contracts and stuff. We can't sell that computer without knowing what he left on it."

"Okay," Debra said. She blew on her coffee. "That sounds fair. Is that what you wanted to show me?"

"No, not exactly. Sort of related, though." Lori took a gulp of coffee, didn't react when it burnt her tongue and throat. "Come around here. I'll show you on the TV."

She hurried around the corner and started picking up remote controls. There were seven laid out on the coffee table. They were the only things in the room not coated in dust or crumbs.

"The first show Tim made me watch with him was *I Love Lucy*," she said.

"His grandfather used to watch that with him when he was little," Debra said. "The two of them would laugh themselves stupid. I never found it all that funny."

"It still made him laugh, even though he'd seen it over and over. But that wasn't why he wanted to show it to me. He said it was the reason he got into sound design. We watched a few episodes so that I could hear how the husband laughs. They were husband and wife in real life, you know. He loved telling me stuff like that." She took a sip of coffee and Debra refilled her mug and came back.

"Anyway, as you've probably noticed, if you've seen it, the husband has a very distinct, very loud laugh. At first I thought it was obnoxious and just bad acting. There's no way someone really laughs like that. But then Tim showed me a bunch of scenes that he's not in, but you can hear that laugh in the background. He's just part of the audience and laughing his damn head off. It's unmistakably him. And Tim always thought it was so sweet, that you could hear how much he genuinely enjoyed seeing his wife perform. That, to judge by that sound, he was the one she made laugh the hardest."

"That's sweet," Debra said. "Sounds like just the thing that he would latch onto."

"When he first told me that, I almost cried. Filled my heart, such a tender thought. Anyway, listen to this," Lori said. She had the TV and the whole sound system turned on. She flew through the PVR menu and clicked play on something so quickly that Debra didn't see the name. A sitcom appeared on the screen, people sitting around a kitchen table.

"This isn't *I Love Lucy*," Debra said.

"No, just listen. Wait until the end of this joke."

Debra stayed quiet but kept her eye on Lori, who stared clean through the TV screen. When the laugh track started, she cranked the volume knob on the expensive speaker unit. Debra winced, spilled her coffee as she brought one hand over her ear.

"There!" Lori shouted.

"Can you turn it down, please," Debra said, setting the mug down, shaking coffee off her fingers.

"Listen this time. Listen to the laugh, okay. I won't turn it up so loud this time." She skipped back a few seconds, then let the laugh track play again. "Did you hear it?"

"I don't know what you mean, Lori."

"The laugh. Listen to the laughing." She reversed again, let it play back, raised her eyebrows expectantly at Debra. "That's Tim's laugh. Clear as day," she said.

Debra didn't say anything.

"This is just the first one I've found. There's also this one," Lori said, going back to the PVR menu and selecting another recording. She played that one, again cued up to a spot with a joke, a laugh track which sounded much the same as the previous one. "Did you hear it that time?"

She dropped the remote on the table and picked up a DVD case. "Now here's where it's really strange," she said, popping the disc into the player. "Those other two are pretty recent. Newer shows that probably used the laugh track from the same digital library. They don't actually record audiences for those laughs. But then, I had this on in the background while I was going through Tim's computer. And listen to this one." She skipped to a particular episode and then a later scene, fast forwarding until a particular spot. She handed Debra the DVD case before she hit play. It was the fourth season of *Saturday Night Live*. Lori pushed play. "There it is again. Tim's laugh. But it's a different recording this time. It lasts a little bit longer, but it's still him. I'm sure of it."

"I don't understand, Lori. First, I don't hear it. But it can't be him. He didn't work on shows like this. I don't remember him ever saying he was making laugh tracks. But even if he did, why would he be one of the people laughing? And this show, Lori. It's from the seventies. Look," she said, turning the case over, scanning the fine print, "right there. 1978. Tim wasn't born yet."

"It's him," Lori said. "I know him. I know that sound. That is him laughing. It is."

"I don't know what to say, Lori. I don't think you should be doing all this work alone anymore. Can I please come help you go through some of his things? We're out of time as it is, and you really shouldn't be taking on all of this yourself."

"You really don't hear it?"

"No, sweetie. I don't hear it. I wish I did. I would give anything to hear him laugh like that. Believe me."

"You believe *me*. That's him. I don't know what it means, but that's him. Maybe he did work on those shows. Maybe he did the sound for the DVD, like a remaster. Maybe someone out there worked with him on something we don't know about. There might be a project that he never finished. Or maybe it's something else, just something left behind. He left so little of his actual self behind," she said. Her eyes stung and she was quick to swipe the wetness away. She snorted back the fluid leaking from her nose.

Debra left, quiet and defeated, pretty much right away. It's true that Lori hadn't meant to blurt it all out like that. There was no context. She didn't have anything to compare it to; that's why she had been spending so much time digging through Tim's computer files. If she had some video or sound file where he laughed, played it right alongside one of the laugh tracks, one after the other, anyone would be able to hear the similarity. Anyone would realize, as she had, that it was his laugh. It was him. She just couldn't figure out how that could be.

How could he have left nothing like that behind. The sound of him. She didn't realize how much of his impact on her came from the noise of his presence. His voice, calling out random things that occurred to him, shouting if she wasn't in earshot. The way he would spew nonsense lyrics to tunes that got stuck in his head. The scrape-shuffle-flop of his slippered feet on the hardwood. The way he exhaled when drinking after every sip. He had devoted his life to capturing tiny sounds, to using those minute aural energies to tell whole stories, but he hadn't thought to treat himself the same way. His story. He hadn't even recorded his own voicemail message. It was just a robot:

The customer you are calling is away from the phone or outside the service area.

Somehow, he had managed to surround her with the sounds of all the rest of the world and then left a chasm where he should have been. And then he'd left her down there alone.

Debra had all but called her crazy. "You can't even hear yourself, can you? We've been trying to get you to go through his things for weeks, Lori. You can't keep all this stuff. You can't afford this place, certainly not if you don't try to find someone to buy all this sound gear. And the rest of his family wants some of these things. His sister wants to go through his t-shirts, his dad wants the movies he remembers watching with him. And now this? You hear him in a laugh track, something that he couldn't possibly have done before he got sick?"

As she stomped to the door, she tripped over Tim's shoes. They always looked so big next to Lori's. Like clown shoes. "What are these still doing here by the door, Lori? Why are you keeping them? He's not going to come through that door and slip them on. Put them in a box and give them away. Throw them out."

Lori didn't say anything this whole time. She just let Debra berate her. "You have to stop looking for him," Debra said and closed the door.

But of course she couldn't. It was all she seemed able to do—not let him go. The only thing keeping her breathing from day to day. She scoured through the thousands of files on his computer, looking for proof of just one time, one instance, where he had recorded himself. A sign that maybe he'd valued and saved his own impact on the world the way he had relished the sound of a footstep, or a car engine, or wind through a small window. She read through all the text messages on her phone, and then checked them next to the ones on his, seeing if there were any that she'd missed. She had the habit of always deleting her voicemail messages as soon as she heard them, to make room for new ones. She hated trying to leave a message for someone else only to hear the recorded robot voice say the box was full. Now all she wanted was some innocuous, useless message from him, asking what he should pick up at the store on his way home or to mention that he was running late. She even found two of her old cell phones but they connected to the same voicemail server, which was still empty.

Pretty soon after it had actually happened, she and Debra had managed to hack into Tim's email by guessing the password, which he hadn't left written out anywhere. There hadn't been much there, no real mysteries. Lori was both relieved and somehow disappointed. There were no surprises. She had known all aspects of his life and if there was nothing new to stumble upon, then his absence was that much more real. Without him, what was there to feed and complement her own life?

She had been surprised to see how many people had written messages of condolences directly to his email address. Did they expect that she would read them, so they were really meant for her? Or were they silent prayers, meant for his digital ghost? Or maybe for no one in particular, sent into the ether never to be read or seen by anyone?

She wondered if she might be able to learn how to use some of Tim's gear and programs to convince Debra. To show that it really was Tim's laugh on those old shows. She couldn't explain how but maybe she could at least prove that she wasn't making it up, that she wasn't just a grief-addled blob. She understood enough to know that there had to be some way to isolate the laugh track and then maybe even pull one particular laugh out of it.

While she clicked through icons, the computer made a little chime noise and an email notification appeared in the top corner. "Tim, are you still interested in: —" It cut off there. She clicked open the browser and found the full message, a reminder from an online shop. "Tim, you were recently looking at: Charley Douglass laff box—would you like to purchase this item?" The image was of a blue pillar, maybe three feet high, and next to it a stack of black square boxes with knobs and sliding markers on the top. They looked like old mixing boards. Very old. The description contin- ued: "Purchased from a collector after the item appeared on Antiques Roadshow. Verifiably the original device used by legendary Hollywood sound mixer Charley Douglass to create the laugh tracks for shows like Andy Griffith and Jack Benny. Absolutely one-of-a-kind item. Working condition. Should be in a museum. $12,000. Shipping not included."

Under that she could see a list of "Other recently viewed items" but they were all repeat entries of the laff box. Had Tim wanted this? It would seem that he had really, really wanted it. He had never mentioned this device to her. But he wouldn't have spent $12,000 without telling her. She thought. Maybe there was something that she didn't know about him. Or didn't know completely.

She hadn't spoken with any of Tim's friends since the funeral and even then she had given polite nods and awkward hugs to everyone else, who all cried while she had stayed stunned and neutral-faced. She hadn't known what to say to them and she dreaded the kind of asinine things they would want to say to her to ease her grief. But if Tim had really wanted to buy this thing, there was one friend who would probably know about it, even if she didn't. Maybe even why Tim had wanted it.

"Hey, Keith. It's Lori."

"Lori? Really. What—ahh. Sorry. Are you okay?"

"Yeah, yeah. I'm fine. It's out of the blue, I know. I guess you haven't been expecting to hear from me."

"No. I mean... It's alright. Don't worry about all that. It's still nice to hear from you, after so long. I suppose I can't really imagine what you must be going through."

That was the kind of phrase she'd hoped to avoid. But she clenched her jaw tight. She kept staring at the image of Tim's online wish list, waiting for Keith to say something else.

"How are you?"

"I've got a bit of a favour to ask you. You're the only one I can think of that Tim might have talked to about something I've found. Something he was working on, or maybe even only thinking of working on but he hadn't managed to get to it."

"Maybe. I guess. I can't think of anything off the top of my head. You said you found something."

"I'm still going through his things," she continued, trying to power through without being derailed into how she should be feeling or where she should focus her energy, "and it looks like he was on the verge of buying something pretty elaborate. Have you ever heard of something called a laff box, with two effs?"

"You mean the Charley Douglass box?"

"Yes, that name is all over this. Tim found some collector and was about to buy it off him."

"Holy shit. Really? Like the big blue thing? It must be worth a fortune. How did he find it?"

"I don't know any of that, Keith. So what is it?"

"It's an old Hollywood thing. Classic. The story behind it is more interesting than the thing itself, probably. I doubt you could use it today, not with anything digital, at least. Douglass was a sound engineer when TV was first becoming popular. TV was so new that engineers had to basically invent machines that could pull off what the studios wanted. Producers noticed that audiences liked shows better if there were other people watching, especially other people laughing. So they had more shows filmed in front of audiences. They could also tell people exactly when to laugh, like at the end of a joke. Even if the joke wasn't very good. It helped them get past dull spots in the script. Soon studios expected to have a laughing audience for every taping, but some shows just couldn't be filmed in front of an audience. So Douglass became famous for artificially splicing laughter into the sound track. He was the only person in Hollywood doing it, was hired by all of the studios, and he carted around this laff box where he supposedly had individual recordings of thousands of different laughs. No one ever knew how the machine worked. He kept it secret his whole life. At some point the whole thing was digitized but the laugh tracks they use now on brand-new shows are still spliced together from those old, original tracks he made in the fifties." There was a long pause on the other end of the phone. Lori had grabbed a pen while Keith was talking but she had only managed to write down the name Charley Douglass, which of course she already had from the computer screen. "Tim was really going to buy that thing?" Keith asked.

"I guess so," she said. Her voice was quiet and she struggled to keep from crying.

"I don't see what Tim could have done with it. Other than just to have it. It's a serious collector's item, for sure, but I don't think that Tim would be able to actually use it."

"I have to go, Keith. Thanks anyway." She hung up, clicked the phone off entirely.

A few days after her talk with Tim's friend, Lori made a decision. She'd done some basic internet research and it looked as though he did know what he was talking about. She found the number of the seller of the machine and called him directly. She asked how it worked. He even played her a laugh over the phone. A single, isolated laugh, pulled from a crowd of thousands.

She came back from the bank, where she had managed to pull all of the debt from Tim's credit card and put it on hers. She kept one of his cards open and let the bank close out the rest. That would leave her with just enough credit to order the laff box. When she returned home and got inside the apartment, she found an old TV/VCR combo on the kitchen counter: a black plastic box with a 10-inch screen. Next to it was a stack of video tapes labeled with masking tape and black sharpie. "Tim - 1987," "Camp Morton," "10th birthday party." There was a note written on a yellow post-it stuck to the counter.

Lori,

This is the laugh I always heard, even after it was clear he'd become a grown man. It was the laugh I heard when you were with him, and I'm grateful for that. It may not sound the same to you, but this is what Tim's laugh will always be for me, and I want you to keep it.

Debra

Lori plugged in the TV where she usually put the coffee maker, slipped in the first tape, and pressed play. It started with a little boy version of Tim running around a backyard, screaming and giggling. A man with a beard, his father, Lori's father-in-law, though she had never seen the beard, fell into frame and grabbed the boy and pulled him into a ticklish, squealing heap in the grass. She hit stop, unplugged the machine and brought it over to the computer desk. She plugged it back in and watched more of the home movie while she waited for the computer to boot up.

Soon the tape ran out and she put in the next one. She could hear hints of the laugh she had come to know but it was still foreign. Too childish. Not like the one she'd heard on the sitcom laugh track. During the brief pauses where the recording faded into different family moments, or when she had to again change the tapes, she brought up the online ordering page. She had the laff box in her cart. She had Tim's old credit card on the desk, but instead she listened to the happiness of a little boy that she didn't think she'd ever known.

THE ASPIRING CULT LEADER'S
HILARIOUS GUIDE TO PUBLIC SPEAKING

[*The following transcript is a record of a podcast episode of the above title, first posted online April 1, 2019, from an unknown IP address. The file has since been shared and re-uploaded hundreds of times. Audio analysis suggests the recording was made on an analog device before being uploaded but a particular device has not been identified. The author, and presumably the speaker featured in the recording, remains unknown. Transcription has been carried out by a further unknown party.*]

Recording Begins:

[Unintelligible rustling, crowd noises, coughs. Speaker is presumably in front of a considerable audience.]

There are many ways to be moved by a holy spirit. Not THE holy spirit. I trust you understand the distinction by now. Not the trinity, father, son, ghost, none of that. But there is a holy spirit outside of us and these extreme reactions you've seen in other congregations, senseless movements and sounds, speaking in tongues, holy ghost dancing, that craziness with the snakes, they are tapping into something real. They're just wrong about its true nature.

The energy. That's the holy spirit. It's the energy that moves people to these bizarre actions, but with the result of improper channeling. These preachers or reverends who do manage to elicit such strong responses do not actually understand what it is they are doing and so the result is mixed, and usually pretty weird. In the larger context, such results are a positive thing but the effect can truly be maximized by one who understands what is happening. It can be transcendental if you know what you're doing. You can lead others to this precipice, the very edge of their humanity, so that they might peer beyond. That's what brings you here now, ultimately, to hear my little lecture. I am here to teach you the proper method. Deep breath.

[The crowd inhales and exhales in unison.]

First, I suppose we should address the elephant in the room. The public perception of our gathering, and of me in particular, has taken a decidedly negative turn. I have been bestowed with the dubious title of cult leader. Maybe you are only here because of that label. I admit that I have not pushed against it. Simple denial is of no practical help. And it can be argued that leaning into this characterization can have some advantages. It draws in more than it scares off.

There is a balance to be struck in accepting this newfound attention and focus. It lends a certain amount of credence. And I do see the logic behind those who would use this term, faulty and closed-minded though it may be. Their attempt is to minimize, to downplay. Because the reality remains the same: people do listen to me. In droves, they listen. Listening is the first step. I started as a listener. Like you. Moving on.

I've never liked the term earworm. Common enough, and certainly evocative. Though what it evokes is quite far removed from what is actually meant. The implied meaning is more disgusting than it needs to be, if you ask me. The image it conjures is rather grotesque. Burrowing. Digging. And where there's digging, something has to be displaced. To make room. Or in the case of things like insects, it is not displaced so much as eaten. And the ears are so close to the brain. But that's not what's meant by the innocuous little term earworm: that ditty you heard on the radio earlier this morning, or even two days ago, that is somehow and despite your considerable annoyance still running through your head. A real jump from the signifier to the signified, if you're apt to delve into the theoretical.

[There are a few titters and chuckles from the crowd.]

What is signified by the word earworm (not the grotesque imagery but the politely agreed upon concept) is useful to our purposes because it indirectly explains what happens when an audience is listening. Music can achieve this effect quite easily; of sticking around in the mind, often unconsciously and involuntarily, even when its welcome is worn out. The same effect can be achieved by certain words, by turns of phrase, inflections of voice. And even whole concepts can take hold in the brain, though this last one is more difficult. Hence our lessons here. The religious shenanigans I mentioned before are of a kind with an earworm. In such an example, the words, but mostly the voice, of the preacher has burrowed into the minds of the followers and produced a bodily result. Most of these are fairly innocuous but there is one form to this religious devotion that taps into something so cosmically true that we should all take notice. Divine laughter. Sometimes called hysterical laughter.

Like speaking in tongues or being overcome with the idiotic notion that you should pick up a venomous snake, congregants are sometimes so filled with the supposed holy spirit that they burst into fits of uncontrollable laughter. Like I said earlier, it isn't the holy spirit as they understand it but laughter has a quality to it that one could call divine. Sublime is even better.

[A loud guffaw, followed by one or two shushes.]

Only humans laugh. Humans are the only creatures capable of it. We may anthropomorphize animals and imagine them to be smiling or making sounds that seem as though they are communicating their amusement but laughter is a wholly human outburst. And that is where things get interesting.

We can still use the term religious experience even though we may not settle on what religion we're experiencing, but divine—or sublime—laughter is a true religious experience. It overcomes one's physical being, convulsing through the whole body and bursting forth, a sign of pure joy and elation. It's a beautiful thing, even when its true nature is misunderstood. Indeed, it is the unstoppable, deafening laughter of thousands that leads these authorities to denigrate me with the title of cult leader. It is because I can provoke this experience, and can lead just about anyone to it. I can show you how to lead others there as well. I can think of no higher purpose. So listen up. Bring them on out here, please.

[The crowd quiets down and there is the faint sound of someone being led onstage. One person shushes while the other whimpers. There is a loud bang, as of someone being forcefully slammed to a chair. The sound of duct tape being wrapped around arms and legs. There is a loud "ha" sound.]

Are they secure? Good.
Step one. Cadence and rhythm.

[The crowd repeats back in perfect unison: "cadence and rhythm."]

The earworm example I mentioned didn't just come out of thin air. The concept is illustrative of the intended effect of certain kinds of speaking, especially when hoping to enlighten your audience. After all, should you find yourself addressing a large group of people, one would presume it's because you know something of benefit to impart. The way an earworm works, largely involuntary but without any inherent violence, is a useful concept for our purposes. Should the knowledge you wish to share be worthwhile, you will need it to run through the minds of your audience over and over, to ingratiate itself into their thinking. Now if you were to just tell them this was your purpose there would be natural resistance. But our brains are specially connected to the ears, even more than the eyes, and hearing allows a way into unconscious thought. Think of the most charismatic preachers of the type previously mentioned, with the tongues and the snakes. Whether they fully realize it or not, that hold they have over their congregants, that sway, comes almost entirely from the sound of their voice. Now, most preachers of this predatory type do know this.

There is a particular cadence, a rhythm and intensity which they hone and perfect and manipulate. The best of them can convince their poorest followers to give up what little they have so that the speaker can buy private jets, mansions. That sounds like an exaggeration but sadly it is not. This is power put to a bad purpose.

The rhythm is most important. It builds quietly, a soft gathering, and then it cascades over the listener. Filling all the soft spots with a kind of comfort, even when the words themselves are harsh. The intensity builds with each cascade. If you were to jump to the midpoint of one of these sermons, the speaker looks outright insane, screaming and red in the face. But they didn't start like that. There was a slow transition to that intensity. This is your model: start slow and build up with intensity. Imagine not the words but the truths of the concepts entering through the ears and gently taking hold, molding the listener's thinking to where you need it.

This is how much religious speech functions and it is so easily used to self advantage. Perhaps the most cynical view is of religion as a kind of linguistic virus, which isn't entirely wrong.

[A deep voice can be heard shouting "amen," followed by chuckles from the crowd.]

Step two. Clarity of voice.

[The crowd repeats back in perfect unison: "clarity of voice."]

Let us not fall prey to the selfish impulses that might lead us to misuse our voice and instead hone ourselves more carefully to our purpose. Let us keep building on the importance of sound and focus on our most important tool: the voice.

The tone and clarity of the voice is important. It is a part of the whole process but one that is easy to overlook. For musicians out there, consider it as important as discovering the tone of your instrument. There is a reason master musicians spend years trying different types of wood, different finishes, no finish, metal strings, cat gut strings. Those listening may not be conscious of the import of any of these elements but to musicians they are all carefully chosen components of their art. Such is your voice.

[There is a slowly building sound of excitement from the stage, from the person bound to the chair. Like a hum.]

Yes, I know. We're getting to the good part, aren't we?

Each voice of course has its own limits as well as its own special qualities. While some personal experimentation and awareness is required, there are a few universals which work best to convey the important message we have before us. Thinking of the ideal voice as an instrument is a good place to start. As an instrument without any kind of enhancements or interference is even better. It is a clean and clear tone, entirely unobstructed by growls, rattles, organic mouth sounds like clicks of the tongue or smacks of the lips. The voice, in more ways than one, is not coming from your physical body but merely passing through it. Your job is to remove as much resistance as possible, allowing the sound full agency over your instrument. Once you are able to feel THAT voice, and you are sure of its purpose, your job is to get out of the way. Allow the sound of THE voice, not your voice, to do all the work. Open your throat, relax the vocal chords. You are in good hands.

65

[The person in the chair loudly guffaws and there is a burst of applause from the crowd.]

Step three. Enunciate.

["Enunciate."]

Here's where it gets tricky. The previous step is all about shedding your physicality in order to let the voice flow out. This one is the exact opposite. You must, simultaneously, use your physical attributes to gently control the direction of the voice without dampening its power. There may be some argument as to whether step two or three should be reversed. I suppose they could as they must operate simultaneously and so whichever you learn about first doesn't really matter. I never said this would be easy.

Real skill and discipline is needed. To carry out these two steps at once requires a level of control and practice not unlike what a master ventriloquist would undertake. Except in this case you would be the dummy.

The voice will come from well behind your own being. It is only passing through you. Think of your mouth, your lips, your teeth, your tongue, as the rudder of a boat or the wing flaps on a plane. Tiny adjustments can trigger huge movements. This control is important for maintaining your hold over your audience. They must understand the words, even if ultimately it is only their unconscious selves that will be able to absorb the deeper truth. No mumbling. No lisping. Crisp, clear syllables. Clarity of voice and clarity of speech.

[The person in the chair is now steadily chuckling, like roiling waves with the occasional "Ha" cresting over.]

The underlying truth is complex enough without unclear communicative tools getting in the way.

Step four. Gauging your audience's reaction.

[All in one voice: "Audience reaction."]

How do you know if it's working? Will you still be self-aware enough at this point? I certainly hope so. Though it is tempting to get swept along in the words, it is imperative that you keep your head. You'll know when it's time for you to give in but you must first usher all of your listeners to this end point. In opposition to what you've been told in other situations, you must put on their oxygen masks before you worry about your own.

[At this point in the recording there is a constant background crowd noise of laughter, snickers, chitters. It was originally mistaken for sound interference but forensic sound investigation assures us it is the crowd creating a background noise. While the main speaker remains audible, from this point the background noise continues to grow louder.]

Hopefully, your audience reaction will begin quietly. Rapturous attention, at least at first. But engagement and increasingly involved activity are the signs that you are getting through to the baser part of the mind, the animal lizard brain, where the voice needs to go. Your audience may start with small shouts of affirmation and agreement. Think of church crowds yelling "AMEN" at the end of the statements they like. This is a promising start.

[There is a shout of "Amen!" and a cheer and much laughter.]

(Chuckle) Well thank you.

You may notice more movement, shouting, clapping, even extreme rocking in place or in some cases convulsions or shaking. These are excellent signs. To an outsider they may seem distressing. But you are on the inside. The very, very inside. Innermost. And you understand what is happening to them. Their minds are being rewritten, their brains rebuilt from within. The earworm is making way. The very last stage of the audience reaction you already know. The laughing.

[Another person arrives on stage, pushing a cart with metal wheels. "Are their arms and legs secure?" they ask. There are some rustles as the taped limbs are shaken, tested. The person in the chair barks and hoots with laughter.]

Step five. Avoid the temptation to be funny.

[Laughter.]

Nothing could be more detrimental to your efforts than to try and hurry along the elusive laughter. Attempting to be funny is the most amateurish move you could stumble through. It's too obvious. Laughter in response to humor is a tension-relieving function. It's a way to force the body to relax in response to stressful stimuli. This is the opposite of our intended effect. The tension must rise without breaking. It must be so extreme that the unconscious mind takes over and opens itself to the influence of the voice.

The laughter we seek, the final stage of the audience's transcendence, is a sublime experience. The joyful, unbridled laughter is a reaction to the full truth of the cosmic universe and our inconsequential place in it. Such a realization is terrifying to the conscious mind and completely liberating to the unconscious one. This is why I prefer the term sublime laughter, for the sublime holds within it the contradictory feelings of awe and terror aroused by witnessing something truly cosmic. Something greater than us. A rare gift. Not a joke.

[From the surrounding metallic sounds, it's clear that the cart wheeled in is covered with medical instruments. There is the whir of a bone saw.]

Step six. Transcending.

[The crowd is noticeably hushed and silent.]

You can begin when you're ready.

[More of the bone saw. It shrieks as it hits resistance. The person taped to the chair giggles.]

We're nearly done at this point and you have almost cleared the way for true contact. Before long your whole audience will be rapturously connected to something of a truly higher order but this means that their essential human functions will be cast aside.

At this point, I will ask you to stand and to form a line. There is no need for distress. Remember that the brain itself does not feel pain. Further evidence of its divinity.

There is one other instance of sublime laughter that I know of which exists in the natural world and does not come from our established practices. It is perhaps a sign of a small subset of humanity more prepared for the next stage of evolution than we are. A natural occurrence of effective transcendence. Much like everything else we have discussed, it is misunderstood by the wider world and is treated only as a disease known as kuru. Sometimes called the laughing sickness. It is often compared to mad cow or wasting disease. In cases of kuru, large sections of the brain material is eaten away, slowly resulting in the loss of motor functions, loss of speech. The final stage of the disease is a kind of phantom, uncontrollable laughter. Is it not possible that the brain is not eaten away, but displaced? Moved aside to allow for the appearance of something else. For it is in the places left behind that the voice takes hold. Losing the reliance on the physical brain allows for a true experience of the cosmically sublime. We need to move the brain out of the way to see it. To hear it. Kuru is spread by eating the brain matter of someone infected. Someone who has transcended. Think of it like a sourdough starter.

Many would call this insane. But it seems that only the insane have a true experience of transcendence beyond the limits of the physical brain. Insanity is not a sign of distance from reality, but rather extreme proximity. The insane have a far better understanding of how the universe really works. And where do we cart them off to? The funny farm! Ha!

[A loud crash, a door bursting open. A flurry of heavy-booted steps. Shouting of the words "freeze" and "go go go." Underneath all of this, still the rising laughter. The speaker is now much harder to hear through all the noise.]

Ho ho ho! But remember, you are the vessel for your audience. You won't see the sublime when they do. This will be the strongest test of your will. You will be left behind, to lead even more multitudes, as I have. For I have not yet seen the sublime. But my day is here. For they are coming for me. And that is why we have recorded this. Heeheehee. I will transcend as well. And after that, it will be up to you. Haha ha. They're coming to take me away. Ho ho.

Tee hee.

[Bursts of gunfire. Laughter turns to shrieks and screams. The recording ends.]

[*Despite numerous inquiries, no law enforcement agency has admitted any connection to the apparent raid that can be heard in the recording. Nor do any public records concerning police raids, large scale disappearances, or even deaths correspond to the events which transpire herein. Investigation of the source of the recording is ongoing.*]

An Aside...

While trying and failing to fall asleep, which is becoming frightfully common for me, I had a thought which complicates a lot of what I've written down already. There are some stories that don't adhere to tropes or that don't fit easily into prescribed categories. This doesn't remove them from the horror genre. It is a nebulous thing: a category, a genre, a focus, a purpose. If we as people and readers are most afraid of the unknown, then at some point horror needs to become unknowable. Conventions must be upended or abandoned. It must spawn new monsters. Only the new can be horrific and scary. New horror must be new. If we keep going into a postmodern theory idea, in order to be truly unknown and unknowable then logically you shouldn't be able to read the most horrific book. It must confound understanding, be unnameable and uncontrollable. The book must be the monster. But this is why I don't dig postmodernism. Eventually, it's just congratulating nothing, masturbatory madness. Weird for the sake of weird, pretending to be edgy. Chaos and nonsense. Experimentation is great, new forms are great. But it has to be reined in at some point.

Sometimes, stories don't fit where we want them to. But more often than not, those stories are all the better for it.

I have more categories to discuss but some of the stories don't really fit into them. I set out with tangible goals but filling a whole book is tougher than I thought and I need to fill out some words. At least 40,000 words. I need to push over that. So let's get these ones out of the way before continuing our little intellectual journey. I hope you like them. Getting the words down hasn't been easy. I find myself fighting against headaches from staring at the screen. Fingers cramped from typing. Like most writers, most of the letters are no longer visible on my keyboard. They are smudged into nothing. Still easy enough to use. The "e" key is the blank one. My "e" key is a ghost. Neat.

DIASTEMA

He sits at the kitchen table, taking the note gently between his fingers. Most everyone he knows communicates through text message or garbled voicemail. But he and Natalie have never resorted to such impersonal communication. He doesn't even have her phone number. Instead, she has left him this note. At some point, not too long ago, she had thought about him, sought out pen and paper, shaped each letter of her message and then made her way here to get it to him, leaving the notepaper folded and taped to his front door. She has impacted the physical world, albeit mildly, in a way that acknowledges his very existence.

He found it on his way out the door, but now he reads and re-reads the words a great many times, letting them bite into his memories, leaving marks.

If only you were here with me now where it is calm and cool, the sharp smell of fall in the air, it reads. The script is precise and elegant in that first sentence. Then the lettering becomes softer, bubbly, every letter built as a loop. *I want you to come to me. Just you. I will wait for you all day. By myself. I'm waiting now.* There was a gap between the blocks of text, a circular perforation. Embossed, like a notary seal. Iain folds the paper in half along the existing crease and realizes what the shape is. She had folded the letter in half and then bitten into it. He reopens the paper, a careful maw. The last words are printed in rushed block letters. *Just you. Come. natalie. 217.*

He will go, he decides. He stands and folds the letter again, closing it up. He slides it into his back pocket, enjoys the crinkle of stiff paper. He locks the door behind him.

*

It was stiflingly hot inside the car. He wiped away a small square of condensation and looked out the fogged window. He looked quickly around the alley behind the gas station. He stepped out, fussed with his hair, tucked in his shirt. He checked his fly. He stretched his arms over his head and stood on tiptoes, like he was recovering from a long drive. He reached inside the car and retrieved the partly eaten apple. He could still see Natalie's tooth marks, the upper and lower rows stretched so far apart, like her jaw had been pressed as wide as it would go. There was a small smudge of red on the skin where her lips had touched, a dull seep of pink at the edge of the white flesh. He had to take two bites to clear away all the marks. He chewed everything away and tossed the apple on the ground. He smacked his lips, which just about masked the sound of the ivory rattle from his pants pocket.

*

Iain reaches behind and presses his palm to his back pocket and feels the reassuring pressure of the folded note. He hasn't lost it. He sees the front of Natalie's building and has the sudden realization that he does not remember anything of how he got here. Has he walked the whole way? This has happened before. Late at night driving alone on quiet roads, the slow crawl of streetlights overhead and the gentle soughing of tires on pavement below, lulling him nearly to sleep, so that hours pass without him noticing, waking in the driveway with no recollection of the drive to get there. Highway hypnosis. It's never happened while he was walking, though. He steps along the sidewalk, picks at a piece of apple skin stuck in his teeth.

Natalie's apartment building is thick and squat, only a few storeys tall. A coagulated red brick, the trim a yellowy off-white the colour of old teeth. An accordion-style metal gate is pulled closed in front of the door. Iain steps onto the landing. There is no list of tenants with their suite numbers, no intercom or buzzer. How is Natalie supposed to know he's here? How will he get in?

He kicks at the corners of the welcome mat, looking for a key. He tips over nearby flowerpots, spilling their contents while he searches the underside for glints of metal or hideaway boxes. Nothing. This is just like her, he thinks. Blockheaded, not even conceiving of the problems he'd have getting in. He's inclined to forgive her, though, as he has done before. That's just his nature, he supposes.

*

She wore something sticky on her lips that tasted like strawberry candies. He prodded with his tongue, felt the edges of her gums, the ridges in the roof of her soft palate, the points of her eye teeth. His lips grew sore from pressing so hard into her mouth. He kept one hand pressed to the back of her neck and reached unseeing for the apple, taking it hard in his fist.

*

Iain is still overturning flowerpots when the metal gate shrieks open and a tall man in a long overcoat steps out the front door of the building, the coat reaching well past his knees. Iain stands, barely reaches the height of the stranger's shoulders. The man slips his hands in his pockets as he steps over the threshold. His tongue bulges against his lips and cheeks. He makes a mouthsound like sucking on teeth already pulled loose from empty gums.

The door does not swing shut but hovers half open. Iain reaches past the man and puts a hand on the knob. As he takes a step, the stranger looks him up and down then smiles. As he parts his lips, he flicks out his tongue, a vicious proboscis. Iain reels back but slides through the open doorway. He pulls the metal grate closed while the stranger stares, walking backwards to the sidewalk. Still he smiles and the ghost of that probing tongue lingers in Iain's head.

*

The bite-scarred apple sat on the console, forgotten for the moment.

"I wasn't sure you'd agree to come out here with me," he said. She gave a polite smile, pulled her lips tight against her mouth without parting them. She didn't show her teeth, which is what he wanted to see. She had pretty teeth. Not perfect. Perfect and pretty are not the same at all. Her two top incisors curved inward toward her tongue. Her eye teeth

78

were pointy and prominent and dominated her mouth.

"I hope you're not disappointed," he said. She broke her smile open just enough to let a slight laugh slip through but that didn't really count as an answer.

*

The apartment building is filthy, the hallway carpeted in the same dried-blood colour from outside, though here it is darkened with flecks of dross. Dried crumbling leaves, torn plastic bags, shards of amber glass, cigarette butts litter the edges of the halls, accumulating in great piles in the corners.

The once cream-coloured walls are shadowed with the build-up of cigarette smoke. A lone bulb flickers overhead. The building's stairwell is straight across from the front door. Iain peers down: the lower stairs are barricaded by broken furniture. He sees all the way to the basement, where there is a dented rust-coated dumpster pressed to the edge of the steps, holding up a fortress of snapped chair legs, split tables, soiled mattresses, pieces of old sofas. The pile reaches almost to the ground floor, right to his feet.

He backs away from the stairs and looks for doors, scans apartment numbers. The first one has none, only a small drill hole where a number might have been mounted, once upon a time. Farther down the hall he finds another door coated in grime, the image of a seven showing through the dirt to the clean wood underneath. One last door at the very end of the hall reads "Management," painted in white correction fluid.

She must be on the second floor, he reasons, and moves back to the stairwell. The way up, at least, is clear. As he climbs, he realizes that there is no banister or railing, nothing blocking him in and keeping him from tumbling into the midden below. He fights the urge to look down. The stairs feel treacherous. He keeps his eyes upward, where he can see a flickering light oozing from the floor above.

The entire hallway is lit only by candles. Hundreds of candles, all different sizes, set on the floor along the edge of the baseboards. They've been burning long enough to spill wax over the carpet and leave clouds of soot on the wallpaper. Other than this, the hallway is quite neat. A marked improvement from the ground floor. There is only one door on this level. The wood gleams in the wavering light. The gold numbers shimmer as though polished. 217. Iain gives two quick knocks and turns the knob, not waiting for a response before entering her apartment.

*

He brought the car to a stop. There were no streetlights, so he left the battery running, the dome light on. The engine pinged as the metal cooled. His keychain dangled, pendulous.

The only other motion was the fidgeting of Natalie's hands. She laced and unlaced her fingers, pulled at the legs of her jeans. She rested one hand on the other. She looked around the inside of the car, at the swinging keys, the dome light, the rolled-up windows, the door handles. He'd mentioned earlier that the child locks were on.

Her eye settled on the Granny Smith apple on the console between the driver and passenger seats. Iain picked it up. The oversized fruit filled his hand. He made a show of rubbing it on the front of his shirt, like in old cartoons, and took a loud and obnoxious bite. The flesh was hard to bite through, the juice too sour.

"I know someone who's gone his whole life without brushing his teeth," he said. "He just eats apples. The way they scrape against your teeth when you bite into it,"—he pointed at the sharp ridges he'd punctured into the apple skin—"works just as well." He took another bite. One cheek bulged out as he chewed. He smacked his lips. He looked at his bite mark again, wondered if he could predict what Natalie's would look like. Where the impression of each tooth would press, where the skin of the apple would split and tear. She said nothing.

*

There are even more candles inside the apartment, enough that the small space is warm and humid. Wet enough to fog glass. She's placed candles along the baseboards, the same as out in the hall, but also atop every flat surface: kitchen table, each shelf of the bookcase. Pools of wax drip to the floor and smack with a hardening patter to the floor. The candles are thick, a nicotine yellow. Stained teeth. He supposes she thinks this will be romantic, somehow.

It takes a few moments for his eyes to adjust to the uneven light. The flickering softens the edges of everything until it all seems moist to the touch. She keeps a great many books. There is a good-sized TV in one corner, though ribbons of wax have spilled over the screen. Among all the candles on her coffee table is a decorative tray filled with tiny stones, each of them mortared in wax. He plucks one free as he saunters past, leaving a gap. He imagines it would taste coppery, like poking at the space of a pulled tooth. He wanders to the kitchen. The microwave blinks all zeroes. There is a short hallway leading to the bathroom, and her bedroom beyond that.

"Why did you want to come all the way out here?" The dropped pebble patters across the tiled kitchen floor. Iain spins around and finds Natalie sitting in the middle of the couch. He can see the back of her head reflected in the wax-coated television screen.

"Jesus, where did you come from?" He smooths the front of his shirt then presses his palm to his beating chest. "I didn't see you when I came in." How could he have missed her? He asks, "May I join you?" She does not move closer nor does she inch away.

"People know I'm with you," she says. She speaks so softly that Iain can barely hear her. She stares at him.

"So what?" he smiles. "Your place is pretty nice, once you get inside. Except for the candles, maybe."

Without moving any muscles, her expression has become severe. The features of her face feel chiseled. The motion of her mouth is hardly perceptible. "Why are you doing this?" He can not see her teeth because she keeps her lips pressed so tight to her mouth.

"You left me a note. And I wanted to see you." Iain stands and reaches into his back pocket but doesn't feel the crumple of notepaper. All his other pockets are empty. He does not have his wallet or keys or any other thing with him.

"Take me home," she whispers. No more words come out.

"You are home," he says. He is still pawing at his clothes looking for his things, wondering if somehow he has placed them all in different pockets than he is accustomed, knowing all the while that doesn't make sense. "Did you take my keys? I can't find the note you left me."

She starts to smile then. She pulls her lips taut in a straight line, tightening. Her cheeks dimple at first and then crease as the line of her lips spreads across her face. The corners of her mouth reach to her ears and only then do they begin to part. At first, all Iain sees is a line of black but then he can make out the pink of her empty gums. All her teeth are gone. Her jaw clicks and pops as she opens her mouth wider. He sees over her tongue, past her uvula, down her throat.

"Jesus Christ," he barks and jumps away. Immediately he feels guilty, self-conscious at his revulsion. He forces himself back to the couch, reaches tentatively for her. "Are you bleeding? Does it hurt? What happened?" She does not answer. She opens wider. He can fit his entire fist inside without touching any edges. "I'll get you a cold cloth or ice or something," he says. It is all he can think to say that will give him a reason to move away from the couch. Away from her empty mouth.

He rushes through the kitchen to the short hallway and finds the bathroom. The door is black-painted metal and has long finger trails dragged through a coating of grime. A blue plastic sign with the basic faceless outline of man on it. Inside is a urinal and toilet without a partition. The sink is missing a drain cover, the metal fixtures are scarred and bleed rust onto the porcelain. There are no linens, only paper towel.

"Shit," he says and spins back around.

She is behind him already, so close that he grazes her chest as he turns. Her mouth has stretched even wider. The back of her head bounces against her shoulders. She opens her hand and lifts it, so that Iain can see. In her palm are her teeth, balanced in a delicate pile. She makes a careful fist around them and then plunges her whole hand into his pocket. He feels her open her fingers, the teeth chattering together. He thinks of grabbing her wrists, of pushing past her and out the door, knocking her down.

She moves first.

She takes a step forward, pinning him to the wall with her legs, and forces her gaping unhinged mouth over his. Iain screams in surprise, a reflex, and he regrets opening his lips. Her tongue fills him. He gags as she licks the roof of his mouth, pokes into the back of his throat. Her lips pull

83

his head in deeper. Her tongue slides over his teeth, prying them loose and then she presses into the gaps of his empty gums. She slathers along the bones of his jaw, making sure she hasn't missed any.

She steps away, her mouth finally closed. Iain hears a sound like marbles in a bag. He realizes she is rolling his teeth around with her tongue. She looks him in the eye as she swallows them.

*

He leaves his car parked behind the gas station but steps around to the front, where there are people. He tries calling to them but can't form words. He barks, shrieks. Their faces become concerned when they see blood on his shirt, even more oozing from his mouth. He screams and they recoil when they see that all his teeth are missing. They back away from him, shield their children from the red, wet sight of him, block their ears as he wails. He hears sirens and screams over them. Police and paramedics take slow and uneasy steps closer. They keep their arms at their sides. One of the cops speaks into the radio. Iain's throat is hoarse, the sounds he makes tearing through him. But he doesn't stop.

As they approach, he reaches into his pocket and holds out his palm so they can see the loose teeth. They watch him take up one tooth between his fingers and slam it into his bare gums. Then another. And another. They rush at him but the screaming gets worse and he grabs another tooth and forces it into the bloody ridge of his mouth.

The report would later say that these were not his teeth, that they were almost certainly female. Finally, one of the paramedics lunges at him and brings him to the ground. The police rush next, grabbing at his arms, reaching for his hands. He drops to the ground and curls into a ball and keeps forcing those pretty little teeth into the edges of his mouth.

Monsters and the Monstrous

What counts as a monster? They are a key element of horror fiction to be sure but we also require monsters in our daily lives. They are a part of how our minds function.

Not to get too philosophical, but the essence of the concept is that a monster is virtually anything that strays outside the norm. By agreed-upon definition, the monster does not fit and thus threatens the natural order. In anthropological terms, the monster is something that appears in myths and embodies qualities or attributes that are endemic to human nature but that are harmful when living as a socialized group. A vampire is not only undead, a perversion of a natural state of being—death—but it also feeds off the living. Perhaps most monstrously, a vampire converts its victim into another vampire. This not only draws capable members away from the social group but creates a new social group of its own, growing the ranks of the enemy.

This same characteristic is shared with other monstrous creatures: the werewolf, zombies. The greatest ill is the multiplication of monsters. Interestingly, this is how a huge subset of humanity has behaved throughout history, namely colonial societies. After initial contact, the amount of settlers continues to grow, until the land which once existed is completely overrun.

There are other qualities more reflective of our living existence which are embodied as well. The classical depiction of a vampire is often seductive, intensely sexual. Can't get more overt than swapping bodily fluids as a metaphor for sex. Werewolves are creatures of rage and ferocity. The sasquatch sticks close to evolutionary lines—a creature which looks almost human but exhibits a wildness and connection to the land we have completely lost. These qualities are not without their allure, which is why we can empathize with the monster. These impulses are barely contained within ourselves. It wouldn't take much for us to lose control as the monsters have.

Quite a few people in my family have dyslexia. Not immediate family but cousins, kids of cousins. Not overwhelmingly, just enough to take notice. Then there are older aunts and uncles who were never diagnosed but always did badly in school or were called "slow," who would almost certainly be diagnosed with it today.

It's still possible to be a writer with dyslexia. It happens, but it would be much harder. I don't have it but I do find that sometimes I read faster than my mind can keep up and I misread what's in front of me. My eyes scan over the words and letters so quickly that sometimes my brain just recognizes a basic shape or pattern and I confuse words that have similar letters. I get to the end of a sentence confused and then have to go back. Then I see different words than what I swear I've just read. They've transmogrified and now the sentence makes perfect sense. It's me that doesn't.

That's what I thought it was at first. The writing pace I've been keeping means I haven't gone back to read the pages very often. My time seems better spent simply getting more words down. Reading them over, sometimes this same thing happens. A sentence, a couple of lines, a paragraph won't make sense. At first, I write it off as the consequence of rushing. I've been typing so fast, there are bound to be typos and sometimes even just rambling that needs to be cut. Kill your darlings, and all that.

But when I go back and read these sections again, slower, they *do* make sense. There are no mistakes. It's just different from what I remember. As though the words have changed, become disguised.

What are they hiding?

I suppose it could be worse. At least I'm not losing progress. Still getting the words down.

Sorry. I got distracted.

If we truly examine what it means to be part of the norm, the monstrous becomes a necessity. The monster shows us where the boundary is, and the group defines itself against that boundary. *Against* the monster. The group is everything the monster is not. In this way we discover that there are teems and teems more monsters than we'd like to think there are. Enough to constitute a group of their own, defined against the normal social order. Through this perspective, the "norm," or the illusion that some kind of normal exists and is to be privileged above all others, is the monster. Welcome to the real world.

There is also the idea of the scapegoat which, while it is not a monster in itself, fulfills the same function as the monster in that it reinforces the acceptable norms for membership in a given social group. The practice itself, when acted out as a cultural ritual, involves imbuing an innocent creature—usually a goat, which you should have been able to puzzle out yourself—with all of the sins, all of the evil produced by the larger group. It is inflicted mercilessly on the undeserving scapegoat who is then outright killed or banished somewhere that they are likely to meet a terrible end, thus cleansing the larger group of these ills. It is the Christ story as a reproducible practice. Societies often scapegoat vulnerable, minority populations such as the poor, people of colour, LGBTQ2S+, the disabled, addicts, and blame them for all of society's ills. This further condemns and marginalizes those people, cutting them off from all support but at the same time reinforcing and strengthening the larger "normal" population.

The most personal definition, and the most damaging on a person-to-person basis: a monster is anything we have managed to convince ourselves is not human. This is not to mean that monsters are not human but just the opposite: our assertions of what is monstrous in other people are always wrong. But if there is a quality which we deem to be monstrous, that person's humanity is forfeit. This helps us understand why so many people could be subjected to such horrific treatment from other human beings. We are designed to deny the humanity of a small portion of those around us in order to assure the fuller humanity and survival of the larger group. We have not managed to correct this defect. Most people are in utter denial that it is even present. It is the larger portion of the population, the "normal" ones, who are the most monstrous because they have been convinced that cruelty is justified in order to protect their existence. To protect their majority. The monstrous is our starting point and there are few among us who manage to break past this original sinful state. And those who do suffer greatly for it.

ALL THAT COLD, ALL THAT DARK

My uncle Laird lives on a cot in a small wooden shed right where the forest starts, out of view of our house. He works on and off as a trapper. He either hunkers down in that shed without barely ever coming out or he's gone wandering through the bush for months at a time. My mother hates that he's there at all. She still looks at him side-eyed most times, but my father insists it's a good thing to keep him around. My mother isn't the only one scared of Laird, he says, and that's a good thing out here.

He drinks and keeps to himself mostly. I can hear him snoring or cursing at nothing in particular if I get close enough to the shed, but I tend to keep a good distance away. Sometimes he surprises me, though.

I like to wander away from the homestead and into the bush. I used to have a dog that came with me but it stopped

93

coming back to the house, probably caught in a trap or eaten by wolves or something, my father said. I was a good way from the house when I saw an old lady out in the trees. Her skin was wrinkled deep and brown but her hair was black like it came from someone much younger. I jumped at first but she didn't really scare me. She didn't come any closer but started talking. Not in words, they were just sounds.

"Wiiii - teee - go." That was the clearest I could make out. She made motions toward her mouth, like she wanted to eat and then she pointed at something past me. A loud rifle shot hit a tree nearby and I spun round and seen uncle Laird and my father tearing through the woods at us. When I looked back to the old woman she was almost gone, a good distance away in the trees. She was fast.

Some time later I was still thinking about her, all alone out there. When no one was looking, I grabbed a loaf of bread from beside the oven, hoping my mother wasn't counting them, and headed back to the same spot. I couldn't find her. After a few hours, I snuck a bite or two of the bread. I wandered a little further. Then I heard uncle Laird call out to me.

"Girl," he said. It made me stop cold, my mouth full, and when I turned, he was leaning against a tree behind me. I'd gone right past him without knowing it. "Shouldn't have come out here by yourself," he said. "What you going after?"

"Just looking for the dog," I lied.

"Mutt's not coming back," said Laird. "Careful what you might find out here instead." He walked deeper into the trees and I ran home. I'd eaten the whole loaf of bread by then anyhow.

There was one other time my uncle went off on his own like that. Came back in the dead of night, tied up. Men on horses paid by the Hudson Bay company had been marching him for days, so they said. I was supposed to be asleep but they was yelling so loud I heard it all. They wanted money, otherwise the company was going to turn him over to the Cree, who'd be more than happy to deal with him. Had to give them something to make up for the mess he'd caused when my father settled the land, they said. The men left once they were paid and it took my father a good hour of cutting and pulling to get uncle Laird untied. He was never allowed in the house after that, but he seems content enough in the shed.

We've had to rely on uncle Laird more and more these last months, though. The fall has been cold and my father is sick. At first, he needed lots of sleep, so much sleep, and now he can barely stand. As the leaves change to snow, I seen him getting thin like grass, his clothes growing empty around him.

I come around the house with water from the well and see Laird and my mother talking. They never talk, not to each other. Information is always passed through father. I couldn't hear at first, except one word Laird says: "consumption."

My mother smacks it clean out of his mouth. "Don't you say that to me," she says through her teeth. I stop where I am, out of sight. They're too preoccupied to notice me. "You're not taking my baby girl out there in the bush with you," she says.

"She's no baby, and there's no choice left now," Laird says. "I know I won't talk you into leaving him. He's my brother and I love him, but I'm not about to sit here and watch his end. He might be the end of all of us."

"He's a strong man. You saw how he managed here, even without you. He kept all that violence away from our door for years before you turned up," my mother says.

"He can't no longer talk, even," Laird says. "That bed is the end for him. You think his soul going to rest if he knows he brung her down into the dark with him?" He points, as though at me, though neither knew I was near enough to hear them. My mother stays quiet now. After a moment she sits on the ground, skirt and apron right in the snow.

"It will be three months, maybe four if the winter stays hard. But she'll learn the land nearby. And you'll need the money by the time we get back. For the arrangements."

"He might get better in three months," my mother says. She stands and storms into the house.

Uncle Laird looks at the ground. "I don't think that's so," he says.

Things turn worse that night. Uncle Laird is allowed in the house but he doesn't sit the whole time. He brings great piles of supplies outside and packs them on a small sledge. My mother brings food to my father's bed but comes back with a full bowl of thin, now cold soup. She won't let me in the room. She sets out a much bigger meal for me. Bread, some of the hard cheese I like, sausage and dried beef, which we'd normally be saving until late in the winter. And some of the soup she'd tried to get my father to stomach.

After a while, she pulls the plate away from me. "You have to learn to control your appetite sometimes. You're like a dog that eats itself sick. You won't survive out there if you keep on like that." She looks ashamed of herself for having mentioned the trip aloud. No one tells me any more than what I overheard.

Late that night my mother flops down beside my bed in the dark. She has a great bundle of cloths and rags. "I wasn't joking about your appetite. When you're out there on the land you're going to have to control yourself." She has no candle or lantern but I can make out the grim expression on her face.

"I know it hasn't come yet but chances are your blood will start sometime while you're out there. It's not anything to worry about. I don't know that you'll get to clean anything once you leave so take these cloths and if you have to leave them, just slip them away out of sight, deep in the snow even, so nothing comes sniffing around. And don't you tell your uncle Laird. He isn't the sort you want knowing about your womanhood." She stands. "This is your last night in a bed, so sleep. And pray for your father."

The morning comes fast and we're away before the dark is all the way gone. We don't say goodbye. My uncle's route goes through two territories and will take us out of Upper Canada and across into Rupert's Land. We're going to clean out traps along the way and eventually we'll meet the fur traders at an outpost where two rivers run into each other. Laird has packed the sledge with blankets, snow shoes, a tent, his rifle, some food. As we start out, we have a few fresh things, cold meat and cheese, but also hard biscuits, dried fish, shriveled apples. Things that keep for a long time. Survival provisions, he calls them. We're going to be hunting all along the way, he says, so we shouldn't need all that. But just in case.

The first night out isn't so bad but I barely keep awake long enough to eat. Laird makes the camp by himself while I sit in the snow. He sets me in front of the fire and soon I'm asleep with a plate of fried bread and bacon in my hands. He leads me to the tent and lays me down on top of the nettles and boughs he's made into a bed. A little later I wake up as he comes in and lies down. It's a tight fit for the both of us.

"Once the nights turn really cold," he says, "you'll be glad for the closeness."

It takes more than a week to reach the start of uncle Laird's trap route and two more days after that to reach the first trap. It's empty but he's not worrying about that. Over that time, we manage to kill two rabbits and a duck. All of them we roast and eat rather than save. He shows me how to hold the rifle properly, where it's supposed to touch my shoulder. I pull the trigger. There's a click but no bullet and he yanks the gun from my hands. "Your mother would never forgive me if I brung her back a killer," he says.

I try to head off into the trees. "Where you going?" he asks. I stammer. "I have to make water," I say. He makes a face but doesn't say anything more. I press far enough into the trees that I can't see him and pull the cloths up from my pants. No blood yet. I wad the fabric back between my legs and wonder if I'll be able to tell some other way than looking for blood on the rags. Uncle Laird stares at me as I walk back to him. He holds still a while and then spits on the ground. "Let's keep on," he says.

The traveling is getting easier. I'm still tired something awful but now I look forward to the dark, the warmth from the fire, the quiet. Most nights, after our suppers, Laird starts drooping and heads for the tent. A few times he's come back out, trying to get me to turn in too but he mainly just falls right to sleep. The night is a thing just for me and I like being lonesome for a while. The cold does more for me than sleep. I wait until the fire dies down, until the embers lose all their heat and go black. Once my eyes get used to all that dark, I look up at the sky. Every night, it's like seeing the stars for the first time.

I never had much thought for far away places or the big things around us. Like the whole of the world, everyone and everything in it. And even further than that, there are things past the earth itself, the heavens, the sun. The empty sky. And the stars. This is what comes to mind in the night out here. This is true dark, like nothing else. I sit in the cold and look up at the sky, to the far fires that have been there forever. I think, wonder, if there were ever fires up there that have burned out. Like the old kingdoms before Gods came to earth, before the earth even was. I feel certain that once there was only dark.

My father used to tell me stories, ones that he said his father used to tell him and Laird. Stories about the sky and the heavens and the earth and God and all the other Gods before him and our special place in all of it. Stories that it seems like people have been telling themselves for a long, long time. And I try to imagine the stories that came even before those. How far back before the first story? And then the time before the first story. And the stars, were they there when the first story came to be told? That first story that has winked out and gone back to dark. But those stars, up there, staying just the same. Unaffected by our stories.

And on this night when I look, there is blood on the rags. With Laird asleep, I don't have to move far off, but it's hard to pull them soiled cloths out of my pants and try to shove down more without tumbling over. I rub some snow on myself to try to clean some of the blood away. It's hard to see in the night and it looks more black than red. Then I dig a few inches down, lay the bloody fabric deep and cover it over. I shiver as I sit back down, cold and wet, wishing to have the fire back. Soon I make my way to the tent and huddle into the warm bulk of uncle Laird. I wish he wasn't right about being glad for the closeness.

Weeks more of checking traps and still nothing to show for it. Some of them are untouched, old bait still there but some are sprung, laying empty. Uncle Laird is trying to make like he's not bothered, but he's not shrugging it off anymore. He starts being more careful with our supplies. We're burning through them too fast and the weather is starting to turn cold. Real, true cold.

The days are long with walking and dullness. I'm hungry most of the day now because we're sparing the food. Laird tries to pass the time by talking, usually about nothing much in particular. "It's good to keep talking when you're in the bush," he says. "Keeps bears away because they spook easy. Not so much in wintertime, though. When they're hibernating." He eyes me suspiciously.

"What was the name of that dog you had?" he asks.

"What dog?"

"The one you went after by yourself in the woods," he says. I try to take a step around but he won't let me by.

"I don't remember," I say.

"You weren't going after that mutt. He'd been gone for ages already. What were you doing out there?"

"That woman I saw. That you and father chased away." Laird looks at the ground quick and then meets my eye. "Did she get away?"

"Me and your dad didn't get her, if that's what you mean. But it's hard land for someone out there all alone."

"Did you know her?"

"I know about her people. You remember when those men brought me back to the house? All tied up."

I say nothing but nod yes.

"A few stragglers from one of the tribes kept coming back, poking around the land. I had to run them off. They weren't scared enough of just your father to leave for good." He turns and begins to walk again. "Where all the rest went, I don't know. Don't seem to matter none. Though looks like there are still some won't leave the place be."

There is a long quiet before he speaks again. I think he doesn't like the quiet. "She said something to you, didn't she?"

"Words I didn't know," I say.

"Wendigo," Laird says.

"That's not what it sounded like."

100

"I told you I knew about her people. She said wendigo."

I've learned there's not much use in arguing with men like my father or Laird.

"You ever hear what a wendigo is?" he asks. "It's an old story, the different tribes tell it all the same, mostly. It's a hungry spirit that eats people lost in the woods. It has antlers like a stag. Stands taller than three or four men put together. Deadly thin. Every time a wendigo eats it stretches even taller, longer, so that it's always gaunt and thin. Starving forever."

"Why would she say that to me?"

"Maybe she wasn't saying it to you."

It's hard to keep track of the days out here. They all bleed into each other. It's been more than a month. Maybe even two, walking into the cold. Still nothing in the traps. No furs or meat. They aren't empty anymore, though. We came across one just now, the metal jaws broken into pieces and strewn across the snow. Huge spurts of gore and blood. But no flesh. Like a taunt.

The red is harsh to look at, after so long of seeing only white. But it rumbles my stomach. Something deep inside me stirs. I know that blood should mean food. And then it comes to me. We haven't seen any creature, alive or dead, in an unnaturally long time.

The mess of the traps is too much for Laird and he roars. He screams and curses into the sky.

"Who did this? Thief! Rubbing my nose in it!" he shouts. He picks up the pieces of metal and throws them, rakes his fingers through red and pink snow. He kicks at a large hunk of iron sticking out of the ground and howls in pain. It cuts through to his leg and falls he hard on his duff. He breathes loud and ragged.

My cheeks hurt from the cold. When I flex my fingers inside my heavy mittens I can feel the cracks on my dry knuckles open up, sweat getting in the cuts. Cold and sweaty and stinging all at once.

From where he sits, Laird reaches out and runs his hand through the red mess again and then sucks the bloody snow off his fingers. "I don't mean to scare you," he says. "Nothing for it but to press on. When we meet some other traders, I'll get it out of them who did this."

We do our best to spread out our remaining food as far as it can go. We peel the bark off trees and boil it to make tea. We drink as much of it as our stomachs will hold, hoping to quiet the growls. The hard biscuits we brought have gone soft and blue with mould. Moisture from freezing in the cold and melting beside the fire. All the survival provisions we brought, though, I don't think they keep any fresher than regular food. You're just stuck eating them anyway, once they're all you have left.

My lips are chapped even worse than my knuckles. I'm always licking at them, which makes them chap worse. The hours and days are hard to tell apart now, as though time is getting away from us. Leaving us behind.

After who knows how many of these blurry, smeared-together days, we come to a spot where two rivers meet. There is no town. No outpost. But it does seem as though it's a place where a great many things meet. Snow and frozen water and blank sky overhead. The tree line is far in the distance. I can see it across the flat and empty land. No living things at all.

"Where is it?" Laird shrieks. This frenzy is worse than the one before. He looks as though he may rip his own arms out.

"I've come this way dozens of times. Dozens! It's here. *It should be here*." I believe him. He kicks away at the snow, searching for the ice underneath. "Here's the river," he says. "We're right on top of it. But there's nothing here. They

102

wouldn't just leave. It was almost a god-damned city. It's like it was never here at all. It's all gone!"

Though I can't see it, I feel this city he mentions. A large fort. Many traders, some from the Hudson's Bay, more from the First Peoples. They have come from very far. I look out and see nothing, no living things, and yet I can feel where they should be. It's as though Laird and I have slipped under a sheet of ice, all the life I feel on the top, us stuck underneath. We're on the side with nothing, just empty air and snow and cold. And we have been drifting deeper for a long while. Ever since the empty traps, something's been leading us farther in. Leading and following us. This deep, though. Nothing has ever been here before.

Laird screams more. First cursing and then just roars. He slumps to the ground. Looks up at the blank, white sky. "We'll wait here until dark," he says. "The stars," he says, pointing. The constellations will show us where we are. Get us back on course."

I don't say anything, but I know it won't work. Though I'm not upset. I don't mind it here, so far.

We make camp in the middle of the wide clearing. Laird insists on keeping the fire away from the trees and out in the open, where anyone who might come along will see us. This leaves us open to the full force of the wind. The gusts are so bad that we can't get the tent to stay up. We dig a small pit in the snow for the fire, deep enough that the tiny flames don't blow out. They don't give off much warmth. Uncle Laird turns his face away and inches closer, trying to warm his back and his coat singes and catches and I have to stomp him out. Overhead the dark grows and spreads until it's all black.

After a long while, hours maybe, Laird is slumped over in the snow, snoring. A dull moon shines but no stars. The fire is long burnt out, my eyes adjusted to the dark. I press my fingernails into the heel of my hand. Hard. The pain keeps me alert. I chew at my dry lips, pulling away thin strands of skin until I can taste the rawness underneath. When I am sure uncle Laird will not wake up, slow and quiet I move away and pull the rags from between my legs. This is the most blood yet, dark under the moonlight. There are clumps and clots cradled in the cloth. Like when I seen the gore-spattered traps, my stomach rumbles; something primal awakened by the blood. Before I can think I've shoved the cloths to my mouth. I gobble at the clots first and then suck the liquid blood out of the fabric. I put them back into my pants, wet now with spit. My stomach is a little quieter. I put handfuls of snow in my mouth, hoping it will wash out the copper taste, the shame from my tongue.

And though it is a great distance away, I see something at the very edge of the tree line. I see the antlers first, can barely make them out against the tangle of empty branches. Then I see the rising mist of hot breath. It could be a deer coming out of the forest, the first living creature either me or Laird has seen in ages, but the antlers reach so high. I can't imagine an animal so tall. Or so still. As though it isn't even there.

I stare a long time, trying not to wake my uncle. I hold my breath. And then, out there in the dark, it blinks. It snuffs a great burst of air and rears even taller as it turns and slinks back into the trees. I sit, unmoving. Eventually the dark begins to lighten and there is only blinding sun reflecting off the snow.

Laird awakens confused and sluggish. He looks around and I can see the memories building on his face. Where we are, where we should be, and how far apart those two things are. Before too long, his purpose returns. We'll keep out in the open and we're sure to find someone eventually, or someone will see us. So we start walking again.

The sun lasts unnaturally long. It seems we are days and days walking but the light never dims. The sun never moves across the sky but hovers, looking down with menace. Or indifference. Which of those is worse?

Finally neither of us can walk any further and we stop for rest. Fall asleep in the daytime with our arms over our faces to block out the light, and eventually awake to pure black. It's as though time has come unstuck here. The dark threatens never to lift. We drift off to sleep again, and still it is dark. There is light when we wake up but it seems as though we have not traveled anywhere.

We can still see the meeting of the two rivers, the trees in the distance. Nothing else. We try again to leave and the same occurs. We make no progress but the cycle of light and dark is unpredictable. No way to figure out how many days it's been. Soon Laird loses all desire to try and leave. He throws the sledge over on its side and makes camp where we stand.

"Someone will just have to come acrost us," he says. He refuses to move from this spot. I find our same small fire-pit. From days before. I venture as far as the tree line and gather wood. We burn the fire in the same place so long that it melts so deep into the hard-packed snow that we have to climb down into a hole to get near the flames. I feel terrible cramps and pain, under my belly somewhere. I check the rags frequently but there is no more blood.

While the night grows to its darkest point, while my uncle sleeps, I look up at the stars. I dig my nails deep into my palms, chew at my sore and ragged lips. Swallow the strips of dried skin that peels off them. Suck at the metal taste left behind. I wait for the loping, eventual approach of the antlered monster. It doesn't come right to the fire but close enough that I can see it clearer now. Even at this distance it towers over me and I have to crane my neck to look at it. The antlers reach so high, the points of hard bone like a cradle for the stars. Its arms and shoulders are covered in thick, coarse fur but its belly is bare flesh turned black by frostbite.

It walks slow laps through the clearing and around the fire before receding back into the cover of the trees. After a time, I feel safe enough to leave the ashes of the fire and follow after it. I crisscross over its tracks, trying not to lose the trail in the dark. I never do catch up to it. Night after night, I follow it to the edge of the woods. I awake to daylight, not far from the fire, the only tracks in the snow from my small snowshoes.

I never tell uncle Laird about it. After dumping the sledge, he doesn't care much for anything. He no longer cares who cleaned out his traps. No longer cares to find the outpost. No longer cares to leave or that the food is all gone. He lies in the tent and waits for someone to come and lead us out. His body begins to take up less and less space.

I pull the bark from the trees and eat it, neverminding to make it into tea. I boil the bootlaces, the webbing from the snowshoes, the ties from our packs, our belts. The leather froths into a gummy paste that I skim off and suck from my fingers, drip it into Laird's mouth as he lies on his back. I gobble handfuls of snow, vainly, to quiet my belly.

Uncle Laird sees me poking at the heel of my hand with a knife, checking the depth of fat the way my father would do to a pig before we slaughtered it. He says nothing, just goes back to the bed of empty branches—the nettles all chewed away—to sleep and wait.

The hunger is getting so bad that it's all I can think about. Eating. I find it hard to talk because my lips are so chewed up. What little I do say is about food. I dream of feasts and banquets.

"I see long tables, heaping with bowls and cups," I say aloud. "There is roast duck and goose and turkey, all shiny

106

with grease. There are bowls spilling over with nuts. Berries soaked in thick cream."

"Shut up," I hear from inside the sad little tent.

"I want to eat all the snow," I say. "All the way down to the grass until I crunch something green in my teeth."

"Shut your filthy, bleeding mouth!" he screams at me, bursting out of the tent and flopping soft to the ground.

"I am eating the trees, eating up all the forest," I say. "I start at the bottom and grow tall enough to reach the high boughs at the very top. And there, suck in huge bites of the clouds and reach past the sky, into the darkness that holds the stars." I loom over my weak uncle, gibbering into his filthy sweat-sodden clothes, a tiny little thing cradled in enormous shadow, swathed in dark points like stars, and I eat and eat and taste blood and meat and feel hair and green things in my mouth, tickling my throat, and I eat up all the world.

It's more than just a few sentences here and there. I'm not mixing things up. They're missing.

There's always some difference between a person's recollection and the reality. The facts of the matter. But there's a limit to how wide that gap can be. Right? It can't simply be boundless, a void to be filled with anything. If that were the case, could reality even be said to exist at all? There would be no tethering so many experiences to any one centre. It would all fall apart.

I've been trying to pay more attention now, since I first noticed there were pages missing. Whole pages. I'm certain now that they are missing. It's not just me. Maybe some context would help. If you knew how I normally work it might be a little easier to understand why I'm upset.

I'm normally a slow, old-fashioned writer so this pace is out of the norm for me. I do use a computer, don't worry. I'm not holed up in an attic with a hundred-year-old typewriter. Normally, I do mostly write by hand, though. Or at least I start writing by hand. I feel that the slower pace makes me slow down my thoughts, better articulate them, as I'm getting down first drafts. Then, when I've got a draft written all the way through, I type it up. Fix mistakes and make revisions as I go. It's slow but it works for me.

So this is the circumstance: every morning at my desk I sit at a laptop, the rest of the desk surface strewn with hand-written pages. It's hundreds of hand-written pages at this point. If a breeze comes through the room, it makes a lovely rustling, like leaves. There's always some scrambling to put the pages back in order, to find the particular ones that should go next as I type. A stitch of chaos.

At first, this is where I thought the missing pages were going. How I accounted for them. Simply mixed up in the mess of how I get the words down. No big deal. They'd turn up eventually, right? But they haven't. I have scenes in mind or alternate wordings that, even as I scoured the pages systematically, one by one, I've never found again. They're in the wind.

I try to rewrite them in the digital draft but it never comes out right. All writers have to deal with this though; to grieve that lost potential. The difference between what we have in our heads and what appears on the page.

Back to the chaos of my desk...

The pages that haven't been typed up yet all stay part of the forest of loose leaves. Within easy grasp. The transcribed pages are neatly filed, first in a box on the top of a shelf right at my side, and then in individual file folders inside a cabinet. As stories come together and are completed, I keep the early draft pages. For posterity. Or backyard bonfires. Over the last months that box of neatly stacked papers has been growing. That's the only dose of encouragement throughout this book-writing endeavour. Proof of progress.

It isn't growing anymore. It's shrinking. And when I read over the story I last typed, it isn't how I remember it.

Not at all.

THE ACCURSED SHARE

For much too long I have been promising myself that I would share this story with you. The details have always been clear and the words to set down I have known for a good long while. But over and over I find myself shirking this task. In truth, I have not known how to begin. The first problem: as what type of story do I present this to you? It may seem a minor, tiny thing to get hung up on, but I struggle to get past it.

It is a horror story that I wish to tell you. There. I've decided. This strategy may strike you as self-defeating; surely warning you beforehand will only suck the horror right out of the whole thing. Better to let it sneak up on you, a dread and creeping thing, unlooked for until quite near the end. Most times that would be a perfectly apt observation but I don't believe it applies in this case. Instead, you will read on knowing that the outcome will ultimately be horrible. You will know this and you will see it happen anyway. And as of yet, there is no actual end to it.

So, "what is the horrifying element?" you ask. What is the catalyst of all this dread that I've promised? It is a story about haunted hair. I suppose haunted is not the best word. Nor is possessed quite right, either. Neither demonic. Regardless, the source of the horror, the monster, if you will, is indeed a kind of monstrously destructive hair.

"That's not scary at all," you may snipe. It may even strike you as silly. I can practically hear you scoffing from here. "I scoff at this," you might say, and fling the pages aside. This was the initial assessment of almost everyone, when it began. In our reactions, you and I are perhaps not so different. But push on a little further and I am sure that you will find yourself drawn in, unable to look away if only because of the utter strangeness before you.

The story is about accursed hair. That's the word. *Accursed*. And it is with the hair that the story properly begins. Like all true terrors, it began unassumingly. Barely noticeable.

We all have hair, after all, and when we begin to lose it— some of us earlier than others—we sometimes go to extraordinary lengths to get it back. Creams, unguents. Do you remember those commercials for spray-on hair? I suppose I've aged myself, now. Perhaps if we, as a people, were not so vain we would have seen the creeping of this particular hair, the accursed stuff, for what it was much sooner.

At the time, it had a natural-seeming progression that no one foresaw as sinister. Where the real hair had been thinning out, combed over to cover an oily bald sheen, there seemed suddenly to be a little more volume. It was in just the right place, admittedly, but didn't *look* quite right. The colour of the new stuff was admirably close to the natural hair but not an actual match. Before long, the blinding glare of exposed scalp was gone, replaced instead by the eye-grabbing swoosh of new colour and texture.

I'm not speaking of disembodied hair. Not at all. There was a person under it; a man, of course. Not so out of the ordinary. He perhaps hadn't aged particularly well. He had soft jowls and a paunch. No one could tell his natural complexion for he was rather fond of artificial skin tone. He wore ties that were too long. I myself wondered if he liked to buy them at big and tall stores, even though he didn't fit such criteria. He just wanted to be "too much" for normal clothes.

He wasn't exactly a public figure at this early point, though he was recognizable. You'd see him now and then on television, sometimes in magazines, when those media still had some popular draw. How he'd managed to attain even this level of visibility is a mystery to me. He wasn't known for doing anything of value but was seen to have a fair bit of money. I wonder still if it was the accursed hair that chose this man in particular for its host, or if the man had stumbled across this odd little being and plopped it on his head with little thought. Maybe he knew all along what effect it would have. If it was the hair itself that made the choice, this man would have been the easiest target. For who else could be so easily convinced that the alien swoosh atop his head was being mistaken for real hair?

That was how it started. Fairly innocuous, an obvious attempt to cope with an insecurity. I'm ashamed to admit how easily we fell for it. It was just bad hair. Why not let him have it? If he thinks it looks good, that it's fooling anybody, why not just leave the poor guy be? We snickered but accepted it.

The story's still a bit goofy at this point, isn't it? Most everyone at the time thought so. Because despite the earlier smirks, which should have been dismissal enough, the man under that terrible swoosh of hair was thrust before our faces more and more. After the emergence of the hair, he did become a public figure, and a prominent one.

The hair itself went on growing, filling out, covering more and more of the man's slippery pate. The colour of the hair became quite lustrous, in an artificial sort of way. It not only covered up the remaining wisps of thinning natural hair but took over the man's whole head, growing into a gravity-defying wave. It became his most identifiable feature, and that fact made us laugh even more. Surely by now he must have known that we all thought he was ridiculous. No one was taking him seriously; he was a clown. Maybe no one said it to his face but he had to know that we were holding him up as an oddity. A buffoon, nothing more. He knows this, we told ourselves. We were just making fun of the hair. And it wasn't the same as plain laughing at him because, we thought, he was in on the joke.

Evidently not. He didn't think it was a joke at all. He imagined all the attention really was directed sincerely at him, that people were listening. He stood in front of cameras, up on stages, and ran his hands through that inhuman mass on his head.

This is where it all becomes truly surreal; people did start to listen to him. Odder still, they began to believe him. He drew followers. Adherents and supporters. This snowballed quickly for as soon as a few people began to follow him, others began to think they should as well. The man under the hair grew bold and boisterous. He yelled and spat, pointed fingers. He shamed. "You are not all that you could be, all that you should be," he taunted. "Let me remove those few that are nothing but drains on you."

Now that I am able to look back in hindsight, it is hard to tell whether the man was behind the words, or if it was the hair. It was about this time that it had begun to cover parts of the man's head that it shouldn't have. The tips of his eyebrows reached past and blended into the hair at his temples. A few people who had gotten close to him claimed that you could see odd, thin little hairs poking out from under his eyelids and one woman told me that when he opened his mouth you could see hair peeking out the back of his throat. Much later, to those few left able to ponder such things, it became clear that the hair was itself a separate entity and by far the more powerful of the two.

At this point in the story the surrounding world events are still somewhere in the realm of natural possibility, explained away by casual everyday cruelty. The global systems where the rich get richer, the poor poorer, as they have always done. Where untalented individuals rise to substantial power without merit. The world has seen such things before.

A few sought to expose the misdeeds which had allowed the unwarranted rise of this man, even as he gained ever wider influence. He was the embodiment of a cretinous and greedy world view, they warned us. What wealth he had accumulated was not earned. Every venture of his had failed. But he was lauded as a pinnacle of progress, a visionary. "He's just a cheat!" screamed those burned by his schemes. "We will lose everything to him." But the adherents, the disciples of the hair, simply pointed and mocked those outlying voices.

The hair promised monstrous and untold wealth to those who would cede power and choice to him. "These others want to take what's yours," he said. "These people lost everything because they don't understand how the world really works. Because they don't work as hard as I do." His adherents flung these accusations of ignorance and laziness back at his detractors, secretly secure in the idea that the hair was sure to reward those same qualities in them.

He (the hair) would make them rich and powerful and all they had to do was give everything over to him. And so the face of the man under the alien swoosh, with inhuman strands of accursed hair poking out of his nostrils, his ears, through his eyelids, became the face of success.

The crowds following the hair and the man (though the man was rapidly diminishing in importance) repeated the outrageous promises and decrees. Their numbers ballooned to insane proportions. Their voices grew louder, the ideas darker. They absorbed the vitriol being spewed down on them by the hair. They deserved more, the hair told them. And they believed it.

They marched through the streets shouting, "We are the downtrodden." They made signs and met in larger and larger swarms. "We are being trampled underfoot," became the rallying cry of a veritable horde. Their rhetoric was preposterous, almost funny, but there were just so many of them.

They fought with those brave enough to say that the words were lies, those who tried with equal rage and vehemence to wake them from this infernal dream that was being spun for them. "Don't believe it. Please come back to us. We need you. You know what he says is not true." This seemed to wound them most of all for any mention of the truth, and how they had missed it, ignited rage.

I wanted to consider myself among these brave dissenters, the ones who put themselves in harm's way to win back the misled. I visualized myself as one of the fighters. But in truth, I was not so brave. I was quiet all the while. Until now, when it is much too late.

In the streets, shouting matches soon became full-blown conflagrations. Once violence erupted, it was indiscriminate: a mass that lashed out in all directions, at itself, at anything near enough to bleed.

116

When the deaths began—and there were many deaths—the hair began to take a form that revealed more clearly just what kind of creature it was. For now it was certainly no longer believable as hair, though arguably it never had been. It exceeded the physical limits of any entity we had ever seen before. The hair changed from being a hideous mane to a dread illumination. The strands were thick like dreadlocks but never drooped. They coursed and pulsed through the air. The hair was now longer than the man was tall and occasionally it seemed that the tentacular strands were the only thing keeping the body of the man upright. He seemed to be shrinking, shrivelling even.

No sound came from the man's mouth anymore, though all could hear the curses and shouts coming from the hair. News cameras filmed it from afar, unable to approach because of the mass of bodies that surrounded it. The crawl across the bottom of the screen read only, "Behold!" as the dread being hissed blame and offered ever more and more wealth and power, if only we would lash out at those among us that were weak. Take what should be ours, it thrummed with bilious rage. It was leading us all to great glory, it roared, though it only ever took. No one received anything and the hair grew and the lands darkened.

It pointed a discoloured strand, thick as a sewer pipe, over at us, the dissenters who remained, and said that we were the reason the massive horde at its feet had so little. They charged at us with teeth bared and arms raised. Food grew dangerously scarce and the hair's dread disciples grew gaunt and pale. So very pale. Their skin gleamed with bare lustre against the dark of the earth and the clouds. We all grew deliriously hungry and the violence grew worse. The hair turned their attention to a dark, viscous liquid that oozed from the broken earth. The value of such stuff, it whispered, would see them all returned to prosperity even greater than they could remember.

You could argue that this wasn't technically a lie, because they actually couldn't remember much of anything. The pitiful things listened and dug the stuff out of the ground and rolled in puddles of it, coating themselves in slick and dark. And when finally there was no food to speak of, they drank the sludge straight from the ground, licked it off the skin of those pressed against them in the throng. Their teeth and tongues rotted to nothing in their heads and they could no longer spew their hatred. Their brains crumbled away, leaving only darkened hollow creatures, unthinking and reactionary, able only to respond to stimuli, like insects. Still they knelt before the great being, now a whole world unto itself. They knelt because they had always done so. The man that had once been the host of the hair had shriveled to almost nothing, lost among the plethora of enormous strands that reached across and possessed the whole world. And the accursed being looked out past the sky at everything beyond.

That's pretty much the end of the story, since it would be the end of us. One could argue, I suppose, that whatever earthly prosperity there had been, before the coming of the accursed hair, was illusory. That we invented it to give ourselves purpose and hide away from the fact that, in the grand scheme of things, we aren't all that important. For even when we believed ourselves to be the center of the universe, we were unremarkable. This business with the accursed hair had merely put us back in our cosmic place. A harsh reminder, a return to form, if you will.

Maybe it's a cautionary tale. For if all of this had already happened, how could you be there to read it? Are the words sent back from the future, as a warning? There you go, scoffing again. I can't blame you for that one. But maybe some things should be taken seriously, every now and then.

Where did the idea for this book even come from? I've been struggling to work on it for so long, I can't remember how or where it started. Or why. I don't know that I ever wanted to write a book. I don't remember enjoying it. The compulsion always nagged, was always a chore. An itch at the back of my mind. And there was guilt for not working on it. The only thing that feels worse than writing the book is not writing it.

Could I have avoided this somehow? Maybe it's just a personal flaw, like an addictive personality. Maybe I tend to do this on my own. Like when I have a drink and see the line where I should stop, knowing I should, wanting to, and then just cracking another beer anyway. And another. All the time insisting that I've got it together. I'm in control. Can I keep it together? Is this the same? What if I gave up on the book? But I know that I can't. I won't. Maybe that's why the book latched on to me.

Below is a paper of mine, from early university on *The King in Yellow*. It's really just a summary identifying key themes. A fancy book report designed to help students identify the basics of literature on their own. Some familiarity with this book will help with the next essay and since this already exists, there's no need for me to reinvent the wheel.

The King in Yellow is an 1895 short story collection by Robert W. Chambers. An incredibly popular and successful novelist of the time, writing mainly historical and society novels, none of his other works have retained any interest. *The King in Yellow*, his first published work, is unlike anything else he wrote afterward.

The collection contains a number of stories with unconnected fantastical, science fiction, and romantic storylines but there are four stories in particular which remain popular and influential today. These four share the connecting thread of a cursed book entitled "The King in Yellow." The book itself is a play which recounts the mythology of a mysterious and dreadful figure known only as the King in Yellow. The main conceit of the curse is that anyone who reads the play is driven insane.

There are short excerpts from the play peppered through-out the various stories with allusions to masks, dreams, the King in Yellow and his symbol, the Yellow Sign, and the fabled land of Carcosa, which is itself a reference to the Ambrose Bierce short story "An Inhabitant of Carcosa." These themes are scattered throughout the stories which centre on characters who have either encountered the cursed book or the Yellow Sign.

"The Repairer of Reputations" is set in a future 1920 New York where the first Government Lethal Chamber, essentially a suicide booth, is opened. The story is an odd mix of futuris-tic science fiction and horror as the narrator becomes abso-lutely convinced that though there have been many wars and overthrows, there remains an official dynasty of Ameri-can royalty, of which he is a member and who stands to reap substantial rewards by their return to power.

"The Mask" is a bit of an outlier since the plot itself doesn't seem to fit with these others except that the narrator has very clearly read "The King in Yellow" play and sees his failing affair reflected in its drama.

"The Yellow Sign" features an artist who is being followed, in dreams and in waking life, by a grim spectre who appears to be a reanimated corpse.

The narrator of "In the Court of the Dragon" is pursued by a mysterious organist who somehow leads him directly into the realm of Carcosa and the King himself.

The stories also share themes of decadence and extrava-gance though it is difficult sometimes to tell if it is a critique or a longing for the over-the-top largesse of pre-revolution-ary France. The mythology of the King in Yellow remains mysterious and ill-defined, perhaps even incoherent but that is the reason for its longevity. Because the figure of the Yellow King and his motivations are only hinted at, the reader can supplement their own horrors to fill these spaces. And other writers have not only used this in their own mythos—Lovecraft was a great fan of Chambers and uses very similar methods in building his Necronomicon and Cthulhu mythos—but many authors have dabbled directly with *The King in Yellow* itself, writing their own stories within and expanding upon the established details of Chambers's stories.

The Dread Figure

(say it with me: "the dread figure")

The dread figure is something with so many forms as to be formless. Even so, it has remained a stalwart and oft-repeated element of horror over the centuries. It can also span a great breadth of subgenres of horror and types of scares, from the completely realistic in the form of a serial killer, to the wildly fantastic like something that usually appears in an H.P. Lovecraft story. These figures, though, are separate from monsters. A different kind of entity, different threat, a different fear altogether. There must be a singularity to a dread figure. They are not one of a legion or species of monstrous creatures.

There are plenty of words now but it's not enough. I can never get down enough words. The compulsion remains. It's worse now. I can't stop.

Even when the words do come, and some days they do, it doesn't ease the compulsion. It stings deep in my nerves, never stopping. I could type, scrawl, chisel, until my fingers are gone and still whatever is driving this need would not stop. More words. Always more words.

I've tried some workarounds. I've cut and pasted words written for something else. I've put in old book reviews, essays. Blog posts. I tried the placeholder text from a website, the templates in the word processor. The book can tell when it's not written by me. More importantly, it won't accept anything written for another purpose. The words must be for it. It wants more.

The rules of a dread figure's existence are murky, hard to define. Not fully understanding it is part of the fear evoked by it. Hannibal Lecter would be one that functions realistically. In the novels, Lecter has no supernatural powers. He is merely a very good serial killer. And though he has been caught, his deeds and how he managed to accomplish them remain mysterious; the stuff of rumors and speculation. Of nightmares. He is a legend, and yet there he sits in front of you. And you, as the reader, are never fully certain just what he is capable of.

Cthulhu would be another, though far more on the fantastic end of the spectrum. One of my favourites, which is obvious by now, is the King in Yellow. These are interesting examples to compare side by side.

Much like Cthulhu and other creatures from Lovecraft's extended mythos, the idea of the King in Yellow has been taken up by other authors who have expanded on the mythology and given divergent and nuanced interpretations of the source material. Like Lovecraft's "Necronomicon," there is a cursed book at the centre: the forbidden play which shares the same title as the story collection. Anyone who reads the play is driven insane and so what is depicted in it is only ever hinted at, gesturing toward something quite grand that is never fully realized. The play does indeed involve a mysterious and powerful figure known as the King in Yellow and so the source of dread is not just the figure but also an object. A text which contains some horrible knowledge that would upset the very reality of the reader.

The forbidden book lends itself a certain degree of dread. Even this book, the one that you're reading now, doesn't function like a regular book. It has a hold on me, though I imagine that feeling is different for you. I think it's assumed that most writers write for themselves. It gives them satisfaction, purpose. I did not—I do not—write this book for me. It's a compulsion I cannot resist. I don't even write it for you.

The book demands stories, words, and takes them in. The words are not for me. I can't even go back and read them. If I do, I feel its breath at my neck, invisible hands hovering near my throat, upset that I am reading. I hope it is not the same for you.

Because of the conceit that anyone who reads the play is driven insane, the stories in *The King in Yellow* exist in a world where the figure himself and the play may or may not actually exist. This is a form of unreliable narration, since if the play did exist, then anyone who read it couldn't be trusted since they'd now be insane. And anyone who does claim to have read it could be insane for reasons completely unrelated to the play. The play itself cannot appear in the fiction because as soon as a reader fails to go insane upon reading it, the basic premise fails. The suspension of disbelief irrevocably broken. So stories like this work through suggestion rather than direct experience for the reader. This is a key to much effective horror. A reader will always dream up something scarier than you could imagine, because only they know what draws out their truest and deepest terror. If you hint just right, give them the right cue, they will bring forth that dread all on their own.

This is getting weird.

The book has taken the pages. Absorbed. Eaten them, maybe. That seems appropriately grotesque. What else could it want with them?

Every day the book tears and shrieks at my brain for more. Fill more pages. And it is hiding them from me.

Unless you have them? What have you done, dear reader? I need them more than you.

MY SON, THE INSOMNIAC

(with appreciation and an apology to Hanif Kureishi)

Alex woke with a start, filled with the half-dreamt image of himself, or a version of himself, standing in the large picture window several floors up.

He had been walking through the small gathering of trees, feeling the dark—so black and uncomfortable. He felt the tall grass brush his ankles and when he looked up to his bedroom window, he'd seen himself looking down. He'd dozed off.

It was already full sun in his bedroom on the fourth floor of a middling condo building. He was still in his clothes from the day before, balanced on the edge of the still-made bed. The mattress springs moaned as he worked his way to standing. After a moment of quiet, he called out to his son. "Jeffrey? Are you still here?" No response. He'd missed him again. Alex sighed.

Surreptitiously, at least at first, he began poking around in his son's bedroom. The teenage boy was rarely outside

133

the room, let alone the apartment, for long, so Alex had to spring inside and search for clues in a careful flurry, leaving everything looking as though it had gone untouched. He was dismayed to see, again, that everything was in place: clothes folded in the drawers, shelves emptied of everything but school books, the supplies on the desk in a quiet, symmetrical order. There were chips and marks in the wood though most of the surface was covered with a desk blotter. He shifted it aside as much as he dared without upsetting the other items. The wood under the blotter was crudely carved into a face. The only disturbed part of the room. There wasn't time to investigate more. The bed pristine and unslept in. It was these oddities which had turned Alex into a snoop. He'd snuck into this same scene half a dozen times now, unable to find any explanation. His frustration led him to be less meticulous. He half-welcomed the idea of being caught. At least it would force the confrontation that he'd been too timid to initiate. He slunk out as quick as he could while feigning composure, pulling the door closed behind him.

He paced the hall between the front door and his own bedroom at the back of the apartment, passing the small living room and kitchen on one side, Jeffrey's closed door on the other. This did little to quell his worry so he dropped onto the couch in the living room, the cushions on either side of him strewn with papers. The coffee table, too, was buried in the work he'd been putting off for days and days. He still had to mark the Senior 2 book review essays and the Grade 10 Shakespeare quizzes. His lesson plan for the short fiction module was only a few bullet points and he still hadn't come up with any questions for the take-home exam on Hill House.

There was a tiny pile of papers he had marked on the floor but he'd been so distracted he knew that he would have to do them over again. It was quiet enough to hear the scrawl of his pen on the page. Every now and then he heard a slight rustling of leaves, as though the air had moved just enough to disturb the papers. He caught part of a stray sentence from one, as the page fluttered up: "his motivations are only hinted at, the reader can supplement their own horrors to fill..." The effect was there—he did look very busy—but his thoughts were hovering over what was going on with his son.

The front door lock opened with a loud pop, tumblers inside grinding as Jeffrey turned the knob. He was actually home early but Alex had been watching the door so long it seemed like days he'd been waiting for it to open. The boy came in, messenger bag over one shoulder and a green leather-bound book pressed tight to his chest. *Again with that book*, Alex thought, trying to crane his neck, twist his eyes in just the right way to read the title. He knew the lettering was recessed into the cover, glinting with gold, but the lavish excess of the font, the glitter and shadow of the embossed print, made it all but impossible to read.

Jeffrey always kept the book pressed against him, never seemed to set it down, and Alex had never actually seen him reading it. Just noticed his son's bedroom light left on, night after night, now and again the soft sound of a page turning and the light quietly clicking off in the morning when Jeffrey would re-emerge.

At first, he'd been pleased to see his son take such an interest in books. Reading was Alex's whole life, his career built around the ideal of teaching teenagers how to read carefully, to see their own experiences echoed in words written down ages ago by people who were nothing like them. But Alex's attempts to coax Jeffrey into reading what had been his own favourite books at that age, or to suggest literature that his son might come to admire, hadn't made a positive impact.

The other changes in his son's personality—the sudden cleanliness, the loss of interest in video games, even the sleepless nights—might have all been related to this new interest in reading. None of this would have bothered Alex if it wasn't that all Jeffrey did now was read. And the only thing he read was that one book. The secrecy over what book it actually was, that the boy was so careful not to reveal, meant that he must somehow be ashamed or embarrassed by it. Alex worried that it was a religious text. Religion was something that Alex never had growing up so he had no idea how to address a moody teenager's questions about faith or the existence of God or the nature of good and evil. Because he was so ill-equipped, it especially worried him that his son had not only discovered a religious text on his own, but that he was reading it with fanaticism. With a singular devotion.

"You in for the night?" Alex asked as Jeffrey walked past him without a word. This had become common as well; Jeffrey rarely spoke unless prompted by a direct question. Alex wondered if he'd have been noticed had he just stayed quiet.

"Should be," Jeffrey said.

"I was about to start supper. Give me a hand?"

"I already ate," his son replied. The words barely escaped through the rapidly closing gap of the bedroom door.

"Make sure you actually get some sleep tonight. I don't want to see your light on late again," Alex shouted. No answer.

This distance, the curt and short replies; there was a sharpness to Jeffrey now that was unlike the son he knew. As though Jeffrey was annoyed by his mere presence. And the changes in the boy's room didn't stop at tucking the clutter away. Earlier that day Alex had taken the kitchen garbage to the dumpster and found a black plastic bag, sharp corners poking through it. It was filled with Jeffrey's video games and movies. Hundreds of dollars' worth, just thrown away. His son wasn't just changing into someone new, but rejecting who he had been.

Alex brought the bag back inside, now hidden in his own closet, but for some reason he couldn't place, he was too nervous to confront Jeffrey. To even ask about it. Or about the desk. Why had Jeffrey seen fit to ruin his desk like that? Why a face? He couldn't puzzle out exactly why, but Alex was intimidated by his son. He didn't want to go so far as saying he was afraid of him but Jeffrey's brooding severity might be coming from a place of real exasperation with his father.

He pushed the papers around in front of him, scribbled with the pen aimlessly, garbled lines and scrawls that he'd have to blot out later. He didn't feel up to making supper anymore. He tossed everything in his hands and on his lap down to the table and stared at the closed bedroom door. Was that turning pages he heard? Or just his own papers in front of him. He blinked with lack of sleep, couldn't remember when he'd last had a good night's rest.

At some point he did fall asleep, though. In the chair in the living room. He'd closed his eyes to rest them and now the apartment was dark, all the blinds still open. He was glad for the brief respite from his thoughts and worries, for the chance to break from the reality before him. Only a soft glow from outside illuminated the edges of the furniture, the outline of the hallway. There was no sound from Jeffrey's room, no lights on inside. Maybe he was finally asleep.

He rose up slow, gentle, but the papers tumbled off and he hissed sharply. "Shit." His back, stiff from sleeping sitting up, popped as he straightened out. He kicked off his slippers so he'd be quieter moving down the hall, took careful steps. He startled as he walked past the kitchen. Someone was sitting at the table in the dark.

"Jesus Christ, Jeffrey. What are you doing out here?" Alex pressed a hand to his chest, felt his heart pummeling. The teenage boy sat at the kitchen table in the dark, eyes open and gazing forward. "Jeffrey?" Alex said. He slammed on the kitchen lights and still the boy didn't move. Alex's stomach sank with a dread worry that the night terrors were back. Or that his son was now a sleepwalker, as Alex had once been. And then Jeffrey blinked.

"Hi, Dad," he said, and turned his head to look directly at his father.

"What the hell are you doing out here?"

"I like it," the boy replied. "The quiet." Alex struggled to read the inscrutable expression on his son's face. "It's nice to not have distractions, I guess."

"Is everything okay?" Alex thought of sitting down but some instinct told him to keep his distance. "You know you can talk to me, right? About anything. We're in this together, you and me."

"It all just feels so...I don't know the right word." Jeffrey blinked slowly, so slowly it seemed that maybe he wouldn't open his eyes again. "Pallid. Like what we see is only out there to cover up something else. Something real. And what's behind that cover is so much more..." He was the most animated and engaged Alex had seen him in a long time. "If we only knew how to get to it," Jeffrey finished.

"I'm not sure what to say to that," Alex stammered. "Does that mean you're not happy?"

"No," Jeffrey said. "It's getting better. I'm seeing things more clearly every day."

Alex patted Jeffrey on the shoulder. He still hadn't moved except for the slight tilt of the head so he could look his father in the face. "What do you say we both go to bed. We can talk more in the morning. It's late."

"In a bit, maybe," Jeffrey said. "You go ahead."

Alex succumbed again to that same intimidated feeling. Instead of ordering the boy to bed, demanding a better explanation of what was going on, he slunk away to his own room, undressed, and crawled into bed. He watched the light from the kitchen bleed under his bedroom door. There was a click when the sliver of light went out but no footsteps. No sound of the chair being pushed away from the table.

From his bed, Alex looked out the large picture window, curtains still open. He could see the small copse of trees past the edge of the parking lot. A little patch separating the condo building from the highway. The branches swayed in the wind, somehow visible against the dark. The stars felt black, and he noticed a sense of something far away and half-remembered. He listened for the sound of Jeffrey going to bed but before long, his own head sank deeper into the pillow, his eyes no longer snapping open, and he was asleep again.

In that space, half-remembering the past, free from his present moment and the mask of calm he struggled to hold onto, Alex dreamed. As all organisms are said to dream, to help them to survive their realities. He dreamed his own memories, and instead of escaping his reality, the dream was an affirmation of it.

Jeffrey was five the first time he'd had a night terror. Nicole snored softly next to Alex, turned away at the very edge of the bed. Jeffrey's room was downstairs but his screams roared through the whole house. He screamed and screamed before Alex even made it out of bed. He raced down the hall, jumping across the stairs to the floor, and burst into the little boy's room.

Jeffrey had a bunk bed, just like Alex did when he was young, and he thrashed and shrieked in the top bunk, all of the blankets and pillows thrown to the floor. Alex reached up to him and said the boy's name over and over. Just whispers at first, fighting to stay calm. His own thoughts blared, he must calm the boy down, but he kept his voice gentle. Jeffrey didn't hear him. Alex said the name louder, tried to hold the boy's small, flailing arms. He just screamed and screamed. His eyes were wide open, the pupils rolling around without focus. Alex kept saying his name. Jeffrey. Jeffrey. Louder. Louder. He shouted over the screams, told his boy that he was safe, daddy's right here. He was home. Just wake up. Tears poured from the little boy's eyes. His mouth was open so wide it was like his jaw had come unhinged, his throat swelling out and shrinking inward with the force of each breath, his voice starting to tear and scrape. Alex climbed into the bunk with him, fighting to get his arms around his son's limbs. It took his whole adult body to hold tiny Jeffrey still, and still he screamed. Alex's ears hurt but he kept saying Jeffrey's name, whispering it, lips pressed against his son's sweaty head.

A tall, thin figure cast a shadow into the room. Nicole, standing in the doorway. Watching. Powerless. Unable to stand anywhere else. Alex looked but couldn't find her eyes in the dark. He just held onto Jeffrey as hard as he could, terrified to let go and worrying that he'd crush him at the same time. It seemed like hours that he screamed. The boy's face and neck turned purple. Nicole finally left, heading for the phone. And Jeffrey's eyes closed. His breathing slowed. And the screaming stopped. She came back with the phone in hand, cautious. The only sound now was the miniature snore of the sleeping boy. Alex let out a breath. He loosened his grip but stayed in the child-sized bunk bed holding his son. After a few minutes, Nicole left and went back to her own bed. Their bed.

In the morning, Jeffrey woke up with his dad still crammed into the bunk beside him. "What are you doing, dad?"

"Just wanted to cuddle my buddy," Alex said.

"Did you cuddle me all night long?"

"No. Just came in a few minutes ago," he lied. He smiled. "Did you have any bad dreams?"

"Nope," Jeffrey said.

Alex awoke to the dark of his smaller bedroom in the apartment, teenage Jeffrey's room silent down the hall. He looked to the doorway, feeling the tall figure standing there still, but all was black and quiet.

"Philosophy department. Doctor Nicole Rustin speaking."

"What do you remember about Jeffrey's night terrors?"

"Alex? Why are you calling me at work? You're supposed to text me."

"That's a pretentious way to answer the phone, by the way."

"I'm hanging up."

"Wait." He sighed, took a deep breath. He should have been better prepared for this conversation. "You remember the night terrors, right?"

"Are they back?" she asked.

"No, it's not that. Do you remember anything from when they happened? Anything that stands out?"

"I'm sure you'd remember more clearly than I do. Why? We've done all this back and forth and you've got custody like you wanted. The everyday stuff isn't mine to deal with anymore."

"I'm sorry for thinking you'd be interested in your son's wellbeing. Enough at least to endure a phone conversation with me. I'll figure it out on my own. Sorry to bother you."

"Okay. Jesus. Hold on. I'm sorry. What's wrong?"

"He's not sleeping."

"And you think it's the night terrors."

"No, you don't get it."

She snorted into the phone.

"There's more to it than that. It's not night terrors, he's not doing anything in his sleep, not nightmares. I don't think he's sleeping at all. I'm up all night lately, just trying to catch him asleep. He's always awake. No matter how early I get up or how late I manage to keep my eyes open, he's always already awake."

"How can that be?"

"Exactly. I thought he was skipping school but they'd have called me. And if he was sleeping through class I'd have heard about that, too. I know all his teachers."

"Have you checked his room for drugs?"

"For Christ's sake, Cole."

"Don't call me that. You've got to be realistic. He's fifteen years old, not your little angel anymore." There was a long quiet. "Meth would keep him awake for days at a time."

He counted his breaths, choosing words. Talking to Nicole still raised his ire. He had to avoid any escalation.

"Alex? Are you still there? Look, you're going to have to consider possibilities that you don't like if you want to find out what's really going on."

"Drugs are what I thought of first, too. I've torn his room apart. There's no drugs. No pipes, baggies, rolling papers. If he was on something that could keep him awake it'd show in other ways. He'd have meth teeth or be losing hair. Bad skin. He doesn't even have bags under his eyes. At this point, I wish it were drugs. At least I'd know how to deal with that."

"Has he lost weight? Does he look different?"

"Weight's the same," Alex said, "but he is different. I can't explain it."

"How many days has it been, since he last slept?"

"Eighteen." Nicole went so long without speaking that he was sure she'd hung up. "Are you still there?" he asked.

"You think he's been awake for *eighteen days*?"

"I've only been counting for eighteen days. It's probably more."

"He'd be dead, Alex. His heart would explode, he'd have a stroke. There's no way."

"It's at least eighteen days. I wouldn't have turned to you otherwise."

"Are you saying that you've been awake for eighteen days?"

"No, I've slept. In fits and starts mostly. I dozed off while invigilating a test the other day. Listen Cole, there's—"

"I said not to call me that. You don't get to call me that anymore," she said. Both of them were quiet for a long time. "Have you had a drink since all of this started?" she said.

He made a show of exhaling into the phone, as though he were insulted at the question. But he wasn't. "No, I haven't," he said, not sure how he'd been managing it, but it was true.

"Good. I'm glad to hear that, Alex."

"Thanks. Look—"

"How do the night terrors play into this?" Nicole asked.

"I don't know if they do. I thought you might remember something I don't."

"Like what?"

"Just what do you remember," Alex said. "What sticks out in your mind?" He wondered if he should ask her to wait so he could grab a pen, then figured if he derailed her now she'd end the call. He waited.

"They started out of nowhere. He'd be fine and then all of a sudden almost every night with the screaming. Sometimes he'd be sitting up straight in bed. Sometimes he'd be thrashing around. Eyes wide open but looking right past you. I was really scared of him when it first started happening."

She took a noisy sip of something. "I remember not being able to wake him up. You were always so gentle but I'd shake him, slap him in the face. Not hard, but it should've woken him up. After a while though, I wasn't scared anymore. Just angry. I used to worry that it would happen when he and I were alone. And then it did. You were over at your sister's and he screamed and screamed and I just closed the door and sat in the living room until he stopped. I didn't even check on him after."

"You never told me that," Alex said.

"Well," she sniffed, "it wasn't a good moment for me. Then there was the sleep clinic," she went on. "What a waste."

"Did Jeffrey ever tell you what he dreamt about, when it happened?"

"You know what the doctors said. It's not really a dream. Telling him about it would only scare him."

"Did you ever ask him anyway?" He wondered if his words were reassuring, or just pushing her to shut down and go quiet.

"No," she said. "I never did." Alex thought about all the times he did ask, grilling the little boy at breakfast. Nicole had shown more restraint. Or less interest.

"Look, Alex, I have to go. There's a department meeting in a few minutes. Are you going to be alright?"

"I don't know," Alex said. He paused, his throat feeling dry. "Sorry. Yes, we'll be fine."

"I'm sure Jeff's okay. The best thing is for *you* to get some actual rest. Take a sleeping pill and forget about it, just for one night."

"Maybe," he said.

"Look, if you really need help, if things get worse, then you know you can—"

"Thanks for talking me through this. Goodbye, Cole," he

said. He waited for her to snap at him for using the nickname again. But after a long and quiet moment, he hung up.

Alex made enough supper for the both of them but ate alone. He fixed an extra plate, covered it with plastic wrap and left it on the table. He didn't bother to knock on Jeffrey's closed door. Then he sat on the couch, looking past the pile of papers to mark, unopened books, the wall at the opposite end of the room, the front door. He looked without seeing.

He jumped at the sound of a key in the front door, startled again as the door opened and Jeffrey came into the apartment. Alex looked down the hall at the closed bedroom door and back to the foyer.

Jeffrey kicked off his boots, both hands pressing the green leather book against his chest.

"I thought you were in your room," Alex said. "How did you get past me?"

"You weren't sitting there when I left. What's the problem?" Jeffrey said. He didn't rush straight into his room, at least. Alex considered that a victory. "There's supper on the counter," he said.

Jeffrey went to the kitchen and tossed the plate into the microwave. Alex stood as the whirs and beeps played out in the next room. He would try talking to him. He would make the effort. Jeffrey checked the plate, set the microwave for another minute, grabbed a fork out of the drawer.

"Where did you come from just now?"

"I was walking through the trees."

"The trees? That little space behind the building?"

"When I move through them long enough, it starts to feel like I'm not the only one walking there. And I can really see the trees, then. And the black stars. Do you ever feel that?"

Jeffrey was reaching out to him, Alex thought, but he didn't understand what his son was trying to say to him. He spoke so cryptically. He settled on sharing something personal about himself, a vulnerable memory that might get them both talking.

"Did I ever tell you I used to be a sleepwalker when I was little?"

Jeffrey looked at him, puzzled. He sucked sauce off his thumb with a loud smack. "No," he mumbled.

"I don't really remember it, but my parents and my sister used to tell me stories. I guess once, your aunt was coming home late. I had a bunk bed, like you used to. Anyway, she comes around the hall and my bedroom door is open, right across from her room, and I'm going up and down the ladder on the side of the bed. Over and over, just up and down. Had my eyes open but she couldn't wake me up. I used to worry that you got your sleep troubles from me."

Jeffrey ate over the sink, shoveling food into his mouth, without pause or breath. He'd set the book down on the table. Alex didn't want to go for it right away, didn't want to draw attention to it, but this was his chance.

"Do you remember when you were little?" Alex asked. "That you had night terrors? Bad dreams?"

"I find dreams misleading," Jeffrey said. "They make life seem real. But when the dream is lost, the life around it dissolves." He smiled between bites, raised his eyebrows at Alex. "Or, at least what we know as life, which isn't really a life at all. I'm realizing how veiled everything is. How hard people work to cut themselves off from reality. From the true experience of their existence. It's as though we all begin with something over our face. It blocks all of our senses, like a caul. A mask with no eyes. And if we could just get the mask off," he said, closing his eyes.

Alex was flummoxed. What was Jeffrey talking about? "What are you reading?" Alex asked, reaching out to spin the book to face him. He could make out the luxurious gold lettering now. "*The King in Yellow*," he said with a sigh. Some relief. No religion in that. Better yet, it was a book he knew. Why read it over and over? "I remember this."

Jeffrey dropped the plate and it clattered into the sink. He spun around to grab the book but Alex held onto it, trying hard not to betray any surprise.

"I read it in high school," Alex said. He wouldn't back down this time, he thought. He would get an answer. "Do you have a favourite story from it?"

"It's a play," Jeffrey said.

"Oh," Alex said. That wasn't what he remembered. He craned his neck to look into the sink. The plate hadn't broken but there was a spray of food on the countertop and across the backsplash behind the faucet.

"I have more reading to do," Jeffrey said.

"You must have finished it by now," Alex said. They stared at each other a moment longer. Alex tried hard not to show confusion or hurt. Or anger, even. Jeffrey didn't show any emotions at all. Despite the earlier urgency, he seemed to have shifted back down to a neutral calm. His face showed nothing, still like a mask, and he kept a solid hold on the book.

Alex started to turn the book, touched the edge to try and open it, finger the pages.

Jeffrey squeezed harder, wrenched his wrist. "Don't," he said. The mask slipping, eyes like fire.

Alex relented and let go. "I'll be out here for a while yet," he said. "Good night, in case I don't see you."

Jeffrey tucked the book under his arm, walked to his bedroom and closed the door softly behind him without looking back. Alex left the food mess and wandered back to the living room, scanned the slew of papers but then went into his own bedroom. He looked out at the small copse of trees at the edge of the building's back courtyard. A space that could be cleared in twenty or thirty steps. There was no wind but the dark branches stood out against the black sky. He didn't understand what had just happened. He inhaled deeply and held it, listening for any sound coming from Jeffrey's room. A few minutes passed and he heard a slight creak from a desk chair, Jeffrey clearing his throat. He went back to the living room and sat amongst all the papers. He picked up a pen and hovered it over the pages, as though ready to get to work. But he kept replaying what had happened in the kitchen, puzzling over the snatch and grab for the book, and then his son's blank expression and the change. Jeffrey's worry that Alex might look inside the book itself.

When everything had gone completely black and dark, he stood, piled everything neatly. The only illumination came from the open door to his bedroom, a straight shot to his window and the streetlights beyond. He trundled down the hall to the kitchen and picked at the food smear now crusted on the counter. He'd clean it in the morning.

Once in his room, he undressed, sat heavily on the edge of the bed to pull off his socks. The blinds were open, the street-light reaching most of the room. He looked out again at the small cluster of trees again. In the dark, he couldn't see the edge, giving the illusion that the trees reached deeper and further. The wind picked up but made no noise. The leaves swayed and bent as though great gusts were blowing past. He'd never noticed that the woods looked sinister, especially in the dark. He couldn't place what unhappy coincidence of perception was giving him this impression; whether it was a badly turned angle of the horizon, the manic and moving juxtaposition of the swaying trees. He listened for the wind but couldn't hear anything from out beyond the window. But he did hear something inside. Very quiet.

Alex found himself leaning inward, his body curling into itself in an effort to boost his hearing. The bed springs creaked and groaned. He hissed low, then stood and hunched his neck and shoulders. Listening harder now. It was a voice, little more than a murmur from Jeffrey's closed door.

Alex placed his feet carefully, trying to get closer without making any sound, without even moving the air around the door for fear that any disturbance might alter whatever was happening in his son's bedroom. The voice, he was sure, was Jeffrey's. He recognized it, though it was something he had not heard since Jeffrey was a little boy: he was singing. A clear melody that repeated, lilting and welcoming. The words changed with every verse, but Alex strained and made out some of the lyrics.

"My voice is dead," he heard, inching closer to the door, "unsung as tears unshed shall dry and die," Jeffrey sang. Alex held his breath, thought he heard the turning of pages. His lungs burst and he took in a gulp of air. A loud creak from the floorboards followed the minor shift in his weight. Alex heard a thump, a heavy book being closed. He was so surprised at the sound that he dashed into his room and slammed the door. He immediately regretted it. He couldn't very well go back and pound on Jeffrey's door, demand to know what was going on, now that he had run away like a skittering mouse. It wasn't intimidation this time. Jeffrey had scared the hell out of him.

Alex looked down into the thicket of trees, safe behind his bedroom window, several floors up. The dark outside, under the soft black stars, was almost too much. There was a figure,

149

though, moving through the trees. Alex moved closer to the glass, squinting to see. He could hear the rustle of the grass, feel it against his ankles. Someone crept through the trees, looking longingly to the black stars.

The figure moved into the light, just long enough to look straight into Alex's bedroom window. To meet his gaze eye to eye. And Alex saw himself—a lifeless version of him—moving through the trees. His face but not his face. The eyes the only truthful part. He tried to speak but no sound escaped. He forced all his might into his throat but made no more than a whisper. Instead, he awoke.

Alex had slept late and found it difficult to rouse himself fully awake. *Shit*, he thought. When had he fallen asleep?

He picked up his phone to check the time and saw a number of missed calls from work. The sound was still on but he hadn't heard anything. He'd missed his first class and there was little hope he'd make it in time for his next one.

Jeffrey's bedroom door was open. He should have been at school by this time, so it wasn't out of the ordinary, but deep down Alex had a sense that he was gone. A heavy feeling that pulled from his core. He caught a glimpse of the trees outside his window, unmoving in the late morning sun.

He ran into his son's room, looked out the window there. He could still see the trees but the window more directly faced the parking lot, the street at the edge of it, mildly busy with traffic. The bed was made, no clothes left out of place. No clothes obviously missing from the closet or drawers, either. As he headed out, he did notice something different: the blotter was gone and he saw the deep gouges and scratches in the top of the desk. The face carved into the smooth wood was worse than he thought. Blank, like a wooden mask. Not just any face. He thought it looked like himself. An Alex mask.

He stared a second longer and then felt an urge to leave the room, as though the thing most out of place was him.

He saw Jeffrey's shoes by the front door, his jacket on the wall hook. Alex began looking for the green leatherbound book. It wasn't in Jeffrey's room. Not on the empty shelves, not in the desk drawers, not under the bed, not tucked under the mattress. He kicked up all his school papers, spreading them further about the room but the book wasn't there. It wasn't on the kitchen table, the last place he had actually seen it before Jeffrey had snatched it back. The book was gone too.

He stepped into his own boots, the smaller ones beside Jeffrey's shoes, and ran out the door. He made his way around to the back of the building and stood at the rim of the little gathering of trees. He looked up to his bedroom window, though he saw no one looking out. A part of him had expected to see someone. He stepped among the trees, swatting aside the low-hanging branches. Leaves and twigs crunched underfoot and he called Jeffrey's name. Soon he had come out the other side, a long shallow ditch in front of him and then a stretch of road. The next condo building a few hundred yards away.

He circled the small stand of trees. It was no bigger than the building's parking lot. And at the ground level, the trees were not dense enough to provide cover; he could look straight through to the road at the other end.

If Jeffrey were to be believed, he'd spent a lot of time walking here but it would have been little more than walking in circles around the same few dozen trees. Alex looked harder and harder for some detail. He didn't know how to look for footprints, but he tried. He looked for anything Jeffrey might have dropped. He picked up small pieces of garbage, soda cans, beer bottles, wondering if Jeffrey had tossed them there. Then he went around the copse again. He did this until the morning sun turned to afternoon, shadows spreading from the trees, the sun high overhead, dipping west. He was stalling, avoiding going home to the empty apartment.

He went back inside, checked his phone for calls or messages from Jeffrey but there weren't any. He tried Jeffrey's phone but got no response. He called the administration office at work and left a message. He'd come down with something and wouldn't be in for a day or two, he told them. He sat at the kitchen table as the apartment continued to empty of light and fill with dark. He watched the front door, imagining the knob turning and someone coming through any minute.

After some time, he did start to relax. It was so quiet. He wasn't listening to hear if Jeffrey was asleep, he wasn't afraid of getting caught, he wasn't worried about some new confrontation. With a twinge of guilt, Alex enjoyed the peace he felt in that moment.

Now it was the middle of the night and Jeffrey had not come home. Should he call the police? What would he say? Had he already waited too long?

He went back into Jeffrey's room and looked at the desk. Alex ran his finger along the rough edges. The face was different. It was unfinished now, the left side of the face undefined, no longer cut into the wood. As though he'd gone back in time.

He wandered through the rooms of the apartment without turning the lights on, holding his phone. He called Nicole. Woke her up. She hadn't heard from Jeffrey either. She thought they should call the police but Alex still didn't know what to say. He managed to convince her to wait until morning. Then Jeffrey would have been missing over twenty-four hours. He promised to call her first thing.

He had a terrible feeling that someone had lured Jeffrey away.

He dreamt of their old house, of slowly creeping down the stairs from his second-floor bedroom, past the kitchen and around the corner to where Jeffrey slept. Alex loved to watch his son sleep. There was something soothing and revitalizing about the idea of it. He could watch the closed eyes, the gentle breaths, and imagine the quiet realm his son was visiting, a place from which he would return rested, nearly reborn.

Alex leaned on the frame inside Jeffrey's open bedroom door. He looked right across at his son, who should have been asleep. But Jeffrey's eyes were open, staring at the figure in the doorway. Alex didn't think that the boy seemed afraid. Though Alex watched through the open door, he knew that he wasn't the figure Jeffrey was looking at.

The boy was mumbling something quietly. Alex couldn't quite hear but watched his son's lips. He picked up the rhythm, bobbing his head along as Jeffrey recited the words. Repeated back to someone. The figure was teaching him something.

Strange is the night where black stars rise
And strange moons circle through the skies

And in the same impossible way of dreams, Alex knew the rest. He whispered, "and tears unshed shall dry and die."

Alex knew the figure had heard him. In the dark he could make out little more than a hooded head, turning slowly to face him. Alex ran back into his own room, pulled his head under the covers. To put something between himself and the figure searching out his face. Alex begged for sleep to arrive before it got to his door. And in the dream sleep did come, and then the real Alex woke up.

In the late morning, the police knocked on the front door. Nicole was with them, two officers in uniform, a man and a woman. Alex stood aside so they could all come into the foyer.

"Those are his shoes there," he said, "and his jacket. They were there when I noticed he was gone."

The police sat on the sofa, pushing aside some of the papers. "Just start from the beginning," they said. "We'll ask for any specifics after you're done telling us what happened."

Alex had little to tell them, other than Jeffrey'd been acting strange and that when he'd gotten up yesterday morning, Jeffrey was gone. They asked what Alex meant by strange. And hearing himself explaining it, he was embarrassed at how it sounded. Nicole backed him up, mentioned how he had called her the other day, concerned. She agreed that the behaviour did seem out of Jeffrey's character. The police asked to look around.

They looked quickly over the kitchen, where the crusty smear of food was still splashed across the counter and behind the sink. They poked their heads in the bathroom, in Alex's room, and then moved into Jeffrey's room.

They opened the closet, a few drawers. Checked the books on the shelves. They saw the carving of the face. It had waned even more since Alex had last seen it—only half the face was visible now. Alex fingered the wood again.

"Did your son do that?" the woman asked.

"I think so," said Alex.

"Was it you?"

"No."

"Then it would have to be Jeffrey. Your wife mentioned that you were looking for him in the woods?"

"Not exactly," Alex said. He led them into his room and pointed at the group of trees out the window. "Jeffrey told me

154

that he liked to walk through there, so that's where I started looking. It's small."

The woman looked over at the male officer, who jotted something down on a pad.

Alex led them out to the spot, pointed to his bedroom window, and even mentioned his dream. "I know it sounds weird," he said.

The officers gave him a card with a non-emergency number on it and said that a detective would be assigned the case and would contact him and Nicole as soon as possible. They told them the case number, and asked that if anything else comes to mind, call right away.

"Your son is considered a missing person. Yours and your wife's concern are more than enough reason to open a case file."

"Ex-wife," Alex said.

"Thank you," Nicole said. The officers nodded politely and drove away. Alex and Nicole went back up to the apartment.

"Where is he, Alex?"

"Is that supposed to be a joke?" he said.

"He's not like this. He wouldn't run away."

"He went somewhere," Alex murmured.

"No shit." Nicole went into the kitchen, looked at the food mess still stuck on the counter. She picked at it with her fingernail and then began filling the sink with soapy water. While it filled, she opened cupboards, peeked in the fridge, the freezer. "What is this doing in here?" she asked, bringing out a half-empty bottle of gin. "Don't tell me we're doing this again."

"Look at the bottle. There's a black line. That's how much has been in there for more than six years. It's proof that I'm in control. If I can't manage having it in the house, I haven't really beat it, have I?"

155

Nicole put the bottle back, turned off the water. She did the few dishes there, wiped down all the surfaces. Alex trudged away. He didn't mind having Nicole in this space as much as he thought. In Jeffrey's bedroom he reached out and touched the bedframe, clothes hanging in the closet. He picked at the mask carved into the desk. How could there be less of a face than before?

"What is that on the desk?" Nicole asked. She leaned against the doorframe, only poking her head into the room. "Did Jeffrey do that?"

"I don't know. He's been saying weird stuff lately about masks. A mask with no eyes. Has he ever talked to you about books?" Alex asked.

"We don't get much further than small talk."

"One book. He reads and reads and rereads one book. *The King in Yellow*."

"So you got him into that, did you?"

"What?"

"You were all into that when I met you. You wanted to teach a whole course on it but the school wouldn't let you do horror."

"I don't remember that."

"I even caught you reading it to him once. When he was a baby."

"I never read it to him."

"You read everything to him. Newspapers, school essays, whatever you were reading. He was so used to the sound of your voice, sometimes he wouldn't sleep unless you were droning on and on."

"You're sure? It was *The King in Yellow*?"

"You don't look good, Alex. You need to sleep. I'm going to the office to use their big printer for missing posters. I'll drop off copies for you later. I think you should try to get some rest." She stood at the door, looking at Alex, for a long time. Then she pulled it shut so gently that it didn't make a sound.

He waited until nightfall and then went back out to the little stand of trees. In the dark, it was harder to see its edges, easier to believe that the wood went on forever, that Jeffrey could be in there. The long grasses seemed to reach higher with each lap of the space. Alex began to zigzag through the brush, pressing his hands on the trees as he went past.

Overhead the sky glittered with the black stars. He looked upward to his bedroom window. There was a light on, someone inside. Alex moved away from the trees and stared at the figure. He expected to see himself, looking down. Like in the dream. But it was someone different. Jeffrey. Jeffrey was in Alex's bedroom, watching. He felt relief and took a large step when the figure held up a hand. Alex stopped.

It was Jeffrey's face but it wasn't Jeffrey. A solid, unmoving mask of his son's face. The figure was much taller than either Jeffrey or Alex. It grabbed the mask under the chin and lifted it away, showing the real face underneath. And Alex was awake, alone in the apartment, in the living room on the paper-strewn couch, the light from his bedroom left on.

Alex locked the door behind him as he came inside. The kitchen was still mostly clean from when Nicole had visited because he had barely eaten anything in the last few days. The stack of posters she'd dropped off was still on the floor by Jeffrey's shoes. The school papers were still strewn around the couch and coffee table, messier now since he had given up all pretense of tidying up.

He went to his bedroom and looked down at the trees again. He'd been through the space three times so far today. His boots were filthy with mud and there were small twigs stuck inside but he didn't bother to take them off. And as he had been doing every day, he went into Jeffrey's room and looked at the slowly disappearing face carved into the desk. There was barely a sliver left, just the very edge of the mask.

His phone rang. He looked at the screen and sighed. He wouldn't be able to put it off any longer.

"Nicole," he said.

"Where the hell have you been? I've called and called, left messages. The police said they still haven't talked to you since the first day they came to your place."

"Sorry. I've been...I'm not myself."

"Not yourself? Alex, our son has been missing for a week. Have you heard anything or seen anything? Did you put up the posters, did you get any calls?"

"Did Jeffrey ever mention the Yellow King?" Alex asked.

"What are you talking about?"

"After you mentioned the book the other day, how I used to read it to him. I didn't remember that, but I do now. I remember quite a bit. I'm not sure if it's helpful or not but it's all I can think about."

"Alex—"

"I know the sleep doctor said not to mention the dreams to him. That knowing what was happening would only scare him. But I asked him. I asked and asked."

"Something's wrong, Alex. Do you need to go to the hospital?"

"At the time, I didn't think that he was afraid to talk about it. But thinking back, I was so desperate for him to tell me. I pushed him. I did scare him. I just didn't care."

"I'm calling the doctor right now. Have you slept at all? Alex, talk to me."

"He said it was pretty much the same dream every time. He was being chased. Sort of. Not like running away, but in

158

a more overall sense. Someone was looking for him." Alex spoke slowly as though he were talking in his sleep.

"Alex, listen to me—"

"A king. He said it was a king, looking for him. That he had been looking for so very long."

"Alex, you're scaring me."

"Sorry, Cole. I'm so, so tired. I think I understand what Jeffrey meant. How we try to keep reality at bay. The dreams seem to be helping." He hung up and took the battery out of the phone.

Alex looked across the table at his young son, working through a bowl of cereal. They were in the old house, the sunny breakfast nook. Alex looked out into the hallway, making sure Nicole wasn't in earshot, and asked, "What kind of dreams did you have last night, bud?"

"I don't know."

"I think you must have had some bad dreams. It sure looked like it when I came to check on you. Do you remember what they were about?"

The boy took a huge bite of cereal, milk dripping down his chin. "I guess I remember hiding in the trees. And running. He kept calling me."

"Do you remember who?" He turned around, making sure Nicole wasn't about to catch them.

"He said he was a king. But it sounded like you, Daddy."

When Alex turned back, Jeffrey was no longer a little boy but his current age, nearly a man. There was still milk on his chin. "It was your voice that first told me of the dream," Jeffrey said.

"Me?"

"You didn't even need the book anymore. You could recite the whole play from memory. You acted it out for me. I loved

159

it so much. I asked if mom could help, play some of the female roles but you never let her. And the masks. We both loved the masks."

Jeffrey's face changed again. He looked much the same but the features became carved, unmoving. And Alex could see a tall figure in the doorway. Its features, too, seemed carved and unnatural but they moved. The mouth articulated sounds that came from Jeffrey's frozen visage, in Jeffrey's voice.

"When we remove the reality, the dream can truly take hold of us in it. But the perception is difficult. The pallid mask must come off."

"What about yours?" Alex said.

And the figure behind Jeffrey leaned closer and whispered, "I wear no mask." And something from behind Alex grabbed his head, sharp fingers digging in under his chin, and then pulled. He woke screaming.

"Alex, are you in there?" Nicole shouted. The pounding on the door shook Alex fully out of sleep. He was on the floor in the living room. His head ached and he felt under his chin where the figure had pulled on his face. "Alex, the police are with me. Let us in." The pounding grew louder, as though someone were bashing up against it.

"I'm here," he said, and the pounding stopped. He had a thought and ran to Jeffrey's room to look at the desk. The carved face was completely gone now, the wooden surface untouched.

The mask had lifted.

There was a loud crack as the door burst open. Alex came out of the room to find Nicole and the two officers coming down the hall toward him. "Why didn't you answer the door?"

"It's already happened. He's gone. He's been out of reach

this whole time. No way back," Alex said. Nicole and the police looked around the disheveled apartment, the papers still strewn around the living room. Nicole stared hard. "Alex, what have you done?"

"I thought I could get him back at first. But he was right—there's no going back to a normal life after truly seeing it. After getting past the dream." He rummaged in the kitchen drawer and pulled out a chopping knife. The police both approached, taking a confrontational stance. "Put that down, sir."

Nicole spoke softly even as her eyes widened. "Alex. Just tell us what happened."

"Jeffrey won't come back now but we could follow him. It was me that first showed him the way. Like you said. I could follow after him. I just have to lift the mask. It's the last thing in the way." Alex raised the knife and pushed it gently against the edge of his jaw, under the chin. He could still feel the sharpness of the king's fingers as he'd pulled at the pallid mask, lifting the dream of life from his eyes so that he could see for himself.

"Put that down, now!"

"Just breathe, Alex," Nicole said. "Come back to me now. Don't go. Not now. Just come back," she said.

Alex froze, the choice impossible, already made. There was no putting the mask back on.

He watched the forest now, looking through the window yet able to feel the breeze. He felt sleep coursing through him, his body refreshing, rest filling him up while his eyes remained open, looking on, aware and vigilant. Watching the trees.

No living thing can exist for long under the condition of absolute reality. Not exist sanely, at least. Even the lowest forms of life are supposed, by some, to dream. The forest out there, not quite sane, as though it were nestled in hills that he could not remember seeing. He felt the grass underfoot, the ticklish wisp of tall weeds above his ankles. A twig snapped, betraying someone else's careful footsteps. But Alex stood in the apartment still, and whoever walked through the woods was walking alone.

He squints and for a moment thinks he can see through the trees. With a blink, the black between the trunks returns and all he sees are the waving of limbs. The stars over the tree line, reaching so far overhead and away, soft and black. He can feel a tall figure behind him. Jeffrey. In the doorway. Humming. The song Alex heard before but this time he can hear all the words. He already knows them all. So father and son sing it together.

Alex continues to sing, though the apartment has grown quiet around him. He looks out deeper to the forest and sees Jeffrey standing at the edge of the woods. Even without words, the boy's intention is clear. Still Alex sings, his voice gentle, and somehow, impossibly, he asks his son, "Where are you going?" And both of them sing together, "Where flap the tatters of the king." And Alex wakes.

It never stops

The Ghost of a Thing

There hasn't been anything especially horrific in my life. I can't think of one thing in particular that might have triggered my fascination. I just like horror. That heightened sense of fear, so high that it needs to be sought out like a fix. When my parents and older sister lived in New Brunswick, their next-door neighbour was murdered. A little old lady. Lived alone. I wasn't born yet so this could hardly be a trauma that leapt over to me.

When I was three or four, I had a toboggan accident that almost severed my nose from my face. I needed stitches. I have weird flashes of memory, of blood pouring out of my face in the bathroom mirror, being held down while someone draped a blue sheet over my face. Maybe they were putting my caul back. Everyone has some injury from when they were a kid.

I do have a fatal disease. Cystic fibrosis. I guess some would call that traumatic. I've been in lots of hospitals. When I was a teenager, I found a stack of sympathy cards hidden away in my parents' closet. They were all about me. Addressed to my parents but in reference to what I had. Dozens. "We're so sorry." "Our condolences."

Like I was already dead.

I imagine it's obvious by now that I have a special affinity for the ghost. The ghost as a figure, as a monster, as a victim, as a concept, as proof of something. As a trope, a story form, a conflict. As folklore. As part of life.

In terms of horror, I continue to be the most disturbed by the ghost. Ghosts can appear in any genre and be used for various different effects but a ghost story, whether on film or the page, is a particular thing. It is a trope with rules and expectations akin to the final girl. In most cases, the ghosts are women or girls.

First off, a ghost is a reflection or lasting impression of something or someone that was once alive. This is an important differentiation. A ghost appears selectively to the living; usually there are people who can see or perceive it and others who can't. Most importantly: a ghost haunts. There is a needed component of repetition. A ghost either inhabits a particular place or carries out the same actions, lives through the same pain, seeks out the same kind of witnesses/victims. It lingers, fades, and returns.

A ghost is most often portrayed as the spirit of someone who has died. In the most common and benign examples, the ghost appears to people it knew while alive, like family members or especially close friends. There can also be ghosts of animals or of lost and forgotten cultures, ghosts of a particular way of life, of an emotion. The key concept would be the haunting, the persistence of a spirit which the living can not only sense but can't escape or avoid.

A ghost story is closely aligned to a haunted-house story, so much so that many of you may think I'm just splitting hairs but there are important differences. While many ghost stories are also haunted-house stories, either example can exist without the other. A ghost need not inhabit a particular place (though it usually does) and the setting of a ghost story need not follow the expectations of a haunted-house story. Similarly, a house can be haunted by entities other than a ghost. Possession stories often mix all of these elements together but rarely is a victim possessed by a ghost. A demon is a different figure that was never alive, or at least not in the same sense as a person who has died and returned as a ghost. A demon is hell-bent (Ha) on causing destruction. They are often portrayed as tricksters and antagonists. Though they may kill or damn their victims, their main purpose is really just to fuck shit up. A ghost is...something else.

STUCK

There were two photographic portraits of Henry James Mitchell taken during his short life. This, at a time when the chemical processes were new and so expensive that few had the means or opportunity to pose for even one. The first was taken when he was still small, no longer a toddler though not yet school age. It was an extravagance upon which his father absolutely insisted: a photograph of the young heir to his promising business fortune.

Long afterward, Henry remembered vividly the day it was taken. His dress clothes itched and were ill-fitting, though admittedly he did look rather smart. Everything was set up in the first-floor sitting room of the large Mitchell house. Henry's mother sat in a tall wingback chair. Once she was settled, Mr. Mitchell approached with a length of thick yellow drapery and spread it over her, making sure that she wasn't visible at all to the camera. Then he lifted Henry and perched the boy atop her covered-over lap. Even through the heavy fabric, Henry felt the bones of her thighs, the strong grip of her fingers and nails. Every point of contact with her a bite.

His mother's touch was an unfamiliar one. She rarely spoke to him and when she did, her voice was always cold. She seemed forever unhappy with him. That is, when she did pay any attention to him.

There was a stranger in the house, a thin man who had set up a little tray next to the camera on its high stand and covered it with odd instruments. He came over to Henry and stooped, hands on knees. He said, "It's not so bad, sport. It's only mid-morning and if you keep quiet and mind me, we'll be all finished up by this afternoon." Henry felt a long sigh escape from his be-draped mother. The man stood to his full height and spoke straight past Henry through the yellow fabric, "You might be a little stiff and feel like you to need to scratch"—his eyes shifted back to Henry—"but your mother will help keep you still. All right?"

Even the sound of his mother's breath came as a surprise. He could hear inspirations and expirations but in a pattern totally alien to him. Just as he thought he'd decoded the mystery of her breath, she would pull a loud intake of air and the indiscernible pattern would resume. Henry found himself thinking of his own breathing, trying to keep his breath level so he could appear not to be moving.

At first all his effort was devoted to holding on to stillness. Though soon it began to feel just the opposite, that if he did not try to move he would forever lose the ability and the stillness would take over.

A photograph works through a special kind of chemistry, his father had explained to him, but Henry thought the stranger's tiny vials and odd instruments looked more like the tools of a potion maker or an alchemist in a fairy story. He imagined a tincture that could turn a living boy to stone, or something very close to it. As though the photographer were using a slow kind of transmogrification to make Henry into the static image that would appear on the finished film. Holding still was only helping that process along.

And that process wasn't being carried out only on him but on his mother as well. The heavy drape provided no protection and she became hard and rigid. Sitting on her spare and jagged lap was growing more difficult. Henry's thighs and tailbone started to hurt. If he strained, he could just hear her soft, inconsistent breathing: now slow little pants through the fabric. His stare was fixed forward where he could see the photographer sitting and leafing through the pages of something while his father kept pacing. Then, as time wore on, try as he might, he found he couldn't hear his mother breathing at all. The spell had finished with her, though it was still working its way through him. If he did not move now he would never again be able to.

He resolved that he would move, even if only a touch, despite the trouble he'd be sure to face. But before the signal had fully fired in his brain and rippled down to his limbs, his mother's grip tightened and a hiss came through the weave of the fabric. "Don't you dare move now or we'll have to start this bloody nightmare all over again." He nearly screamed at the shock that there remained life in her yet.

He did hold still and the photograph came out pretty well. Sadly, this experience would become one of Henry's only memories of his living mother as all thoughts of her were dominated by the second photograph in which they are posed together. She is not covered up in that one. They are holding hands. It was taken six days after she died.

Henry heard about his mother's death by brief telegram, handed to him by the school headmaster. Indeed, all news Henry ever received about his family came by telegram as he only rarely visited home. His father sent the occasional letter but his mother had never once written to him.

Henry read the words,

> Henry -(stop)-
> Your dear mother has passed -(stop)-
> Return home for funeral -(stop)-
> Mr. J.H. Mitchell, ESQ.

As he read, the headmaster continued speaking, something about how Henry would be returning home for other reasons anyway and that he and his father had much to discuss. "My condolences for your circumstances," the headmaster said. "Please make sure to pack all of your belongings. All other arrangements have been made."

"When will I be coming back?"

"I'm afraid that won't be the case, master Mitchell. You'll have to discuss the details with your father."

Henry made the trip home by train as he had done only a few times before. Such a trek was usually reserved for Christmas or other very special holidays, though at his parents' behest he had spent the most recent Christmas and New Year's alone in his dormitory. As he rode on the train, Henry tried to conjure some measure of sadness; his mother had just passed after all. To his disappointment he found that he didn't feel sad at all. His mother was a stranger to him, one that others had told him repeatedly was such an important influence in his life, to his character, but he didn't feel any impact from her. He knew only that she was his mother and that she was not fond of him. Did not seem to like him at all, in fact. She could have been anyone. She might have been caring and loving, cheerful. She might equally have been cruel and vicious and if Henry had been home with her, he might have fallen victim to her tortures. He could fill the absent space of his mother with just about anything.

Henry didn't mind riding the train by himself. At first he'd assumed this trip would feel quite different, given the circumstance, but it felt perfectly ordinary. He saw other children his age but none were riding alone. Once the train pulled into the station he stepped off the platform, struggling to lift his heavy suitcase off the ground. An attendant approached him right away. "Master Mitchell?" he asked. Henry nodded at the stranger. "Your father has left a note that he is unable to meet you at the station and that you can make your way home on your own." He handed a folded piece of paper to Henry and went back inside the station. Henry tucked the little paper in his pocket without giving it a glance and started walking.

Henry did his best to carry the suitcase the whole way, as he was sure an adult would have been able to manage. He did have to stop several times, though, and rest by the side of the road to relax his arms and catch his breath. In his memory the walk had not seemed so far but now it seemed as though he was racing against the sunset. He wondered if it would be difficult to make out the house in the dark. His mother would probably be in her dressing gown already and would scold him for delaying her retirement to bed. Or should already be asleep, uncaring for the late return of a son she hadn't wanted. Or she'd be dead. She didn't care because she was dead. He quickened his pace anyway, not wanting to be on the street after dark.

Once through the front door, Henry heard his father's familiar booming voice but what was being said, and to whom, was out of place with what he remembered of home.

"At this time, Mister Weir," his father said, "I am prepared to negotiate a price for the furniture in the sitting room only. My home is not open for bidding."

"Begging your pardon, sir," said the smaller gentleman Henry did not recognize, who seemed undeterred by the tone in Mr. Mitchell's voice. "I can't help but notice the stunning woodwork and that you have at least two rooms sealed up and I merely assumed—"

"I do not need to tear my house down in order to sell the pieces," responded Mr. Mitchell. "Now, are you prepared to pay the amount already negotiated? Or—" his father noticed Henry standing in the doorway and tumbled over his sentence. The other man looked over at Henry and Mr. Mitchell snapped his fingers to pull the man's attention back to him. "Henry, would you wait for me in the kitchen please."

There was a long hush as both men looked each other up and down. Henry moved slowly down the hall but turned to see the stranger flip open a ledger, scribble something, tear a small piece of paper and hand it to Mr. Mitchell, who folded and placed it in his breast pocket.

"I'll send word when you can expect my men to pick everything up."

"Yes, fine," said Mr. Mitchell. "Off you go, then." He all but shooed the man out the door. The tongue from the door lock clicked and only after a few moments did Mr. Mitchell regain his composure and take notice again of his son.

"Here's my Henry," he said as he scooped the boy into his arms. Henry held his back straight, his limbs rigid. A hug from his father was not unheard of and it had been a long time since the two of them were in the same room, he supposed, but there was an immediacy that Henry had never associated with familial affection. He couldn't have broken out of that hold, even if he'd wanted to. He had never known his father to seek that kind of contact before. Soon, though, the awkwardness passed and Henry gave in to the happy feeling of being nestled in his father's strong, tweed-coated arms.

"Welcome home, Hal," his father said. The nickname was out of place, for Henry's mother had always hated it, but she was not there to complain. He squared the boy's shoulders with heavy hands and then stood to his full height. "I'm sorry you arrived before that buffoon had left. You needn't have heard any of that." He led Henry back through the hallway to the front door where his suitcase waited. "Let's get this up to your room, then."

Henry could think of nothing to say and felt ungainly looking up at his father's face. He looked around at the house, which felt empty even with the two of them standing close together. The doorway to the family's library was covered over with boards and a tarp, as was the door to the dining room. Sealed off, if one were to believe the stranger.

"Come upstairs and see your mother," Mr. Mitchell said as he lifted the suitcase in one hand, rested the other on Henry's shoulder, and led him toward the stairs.

"What do you mean?" Henry said. His father didn't answer, just kept coaxing him up the steps. At the top of the stairs, Henry looked over to where the door to his room stood ajar. His father set the suitcase down and pulled the boy in the opposite direction.

The door to Mrs. Mitchell's room was also ajar. Henry's parents had always slept in separate rooms. Mr. Mitchell led the boy inside, pausing to ensure that Henry entered first. The room was very still and smelled overwhelmingly of flowers. Henry's mother was laid stiffly atop the pristinely made bed, no pillow so that she was completely flat. Her hands were laid one atop the other on her waist, a cluster of flowers placed close enough to graze the edges of her fingers. There were flowers on the night tables, a wreath hanging over the headboard and more tied to the bedposts: lilacs, gardenias, lilies, posies, little nosegays.

Her mouth and eyes were pressed closed but did not look natural. The eyelids were mostly closed and the eyes themselves seemed to have fallen into her skull and Henry could see the white where her lids didn't quite press together. Her chin was sunken, as though while lying dead her jawbone had sunk to the back of her neck. As Henry moved further into the room the flower smell was no longer pleasant and it could not hide the smell of rot.

"It will still be a few days yet, before the photographer arrives to do the portrait," Mr. Mitchell said. "I tried to press him but he claims he's travelling as fast as possible. He suggested she be laid out in the cold cellar until he arrives." His voice grew quiet, missing the booming confidence Henry most associated with him. "Imagine," his father whispered. When he spoke again his voice had regained its powerful timbre. "I gathered all the flowers myself, you know." He looked around the room, the hush settling down on them once again. "They are quite lovely," he said.

"Why are you keeping her in the house?" Henry asked. He pressed the end of his nose with his palm, something his mother would have complained about as she pulled his arm away from his face. "I don't like being in here," he said.

"Nonsense. This is her home and yours. Once the portrait is taken, we'll have a burial and all that. But in the meantime, she is comfortable here," he said, pushing the boy closer to the bed. "Isn't she peaceful?"

"We can still get everything back to the way it was," Mr. Mitchell said. He took one of the boy's hands and placed it on his mother's dead ones, her skin like cold paper. The house was silent with expectation. Henry tried to control his breathing and keep from appearing panicked. "You best

176

give her a kiss now, Hal." Did she sneer at the nickname? Of course not, Henry thought. His father went on, "Soon you'll have missed your chance." Henry did not want to but did not want to disappoint his father. Whatever he felt towards the corpse of his mother was not shared by the elder Mitchell. In fact, his father seemed comforted by it.

Henry steeled himself and, with slow deliberation, leaned over and whisked his lips against his dead mother's forehead. It was cold, the skin very soft. He was unsure if it had been the same when she was alive as he could not recall a single instance where he had kissed his mother. She never wanted him to and he remembered only that she would turn her face away if he approached.

"Let's see about something for supper then," said Mr. Mitchell, moving aside to unblock the boy's path. Henry leaned on all of his willpower to walk out with respect and deference, rather than charging out at a dead run.

That night Henry lay awake with his eyes open, trying not to glance at the bedroom down the hall where he knew his mother lay with her eyes slowly sinking into her head. Mr. Mitchell insisted on keeping her door open and Henry could see out the doorway of his own room, down the hall, and just make out the shape of the foot of her bed in the dark. The smell of the flowers grew worse at night as the house released whatever heat it had absorbed during the day. Henry couldn't help but watch her doorway, convinced that she was on the verge of getting up and walking about, though he prayed with all his might that no such thing could happen. He tried turning and facing the wall but not being able to see into her room was even worse. Even more out of the question was to make his way out of bed and pull one of the doors closed, either hers or his.

In the dark, he couldn't see any detail. He squinted and tried to focus his eyes and convince himself that he could see more than just the shape of her bed, that he could see flower petals sloughing to the ground, the blankets rustling the tiniest bit. The mound of covers over her feet moving, then retreating as she sat up, and finally the blankets being tossed aside onto the ground. The smell of flowers completely faded and Henry smelled only the stink of someone dead. Some woman he didn't know that everyone insisted on calling his mother. He had not lived under this roof with her, did not see how she spent her time. All he knew for sure was that she hadn't wanted a son, or at least didn't want him. For all he knew, she could have been a cruel woman, or a witch, hellbent on ridding her house of him. Some spell that would snap him out of existence. And if she could do that, she would also be able to rise out of that bed, as she was doing now. In the terrible darkness, she would be at his doorway before long, flowers jutting out of her dress and hair. Her jaw, still unhinged, bouncing down to her neck. She would turn side to side but her eyes were sunken, still mostly closed. She would lift her blue hands to her face and push the eyelids up, her pupils twitching. Her eyes trying to roll around in her dried-out head. And then she would see him. Her eyes focused.

Henry's eyes opened as he jolted himself awake, out of breath. He could not see in the full darkness. He blinked, slowly adjusting out of sleep. The house was still, no one in his room, no one in his doorway. He looked down the hall and through his mother's open door, the bare shape of the bed unchanged. She lay in just the same place.

A few days later, Henry's father woke him early in the morning. "We'll be doing the portrait this morning and afternoon, Hal. Get dressed," he said.

Henry slipped on his pressed vest and trousers one at a time. Then he did up his tie and uncomfortable shoes. Once dressed he sat on the edge of the bed and waited. His father came out of his own room, saw him there, and pulled the boy down the stairs along with him. "Get something to eat or you'll be faint before we're done," Mr. Mitchell said and went to answer the door.

Henry couldn't eat anything. He could hear things being moved around in the next room, the sitting room, and soft murmurings as his father and the photographer exchanged pleasantries.

"How many days has it been?" said the other voice.

"Six," said his father's voice. Their footsteps were leading back toward the stairs.

"She won't be stiff anymore." The pair of men stopped moving. "Forgive my bluntness, mister Mitchell. It may be difficult to keep her propped up, is what I meant. I'm prepared for it, though. I've something of a stand."

After a pause, the steps resumed. Henry poked his head out of the kitchen and watched his father and the other man reach the top of the stairs, then cross the hall into his mother's room. "Go on into the sitting room, Hal," his father called down.

The sitting room was rearranged, the chesterfield dragged to the middle of the floor, the camera on its stand just opposite. Behind it was a bookcase, which hadn't been moved, and Henry found placed on it the older photograph of himself sitting on his mother's lap. He remembered the sickly yellow drape over her, though now everything had a faded tinge of brown. His own face was a pale cream colour, the details of his features blurred and dull. He could make out every facet of his mother's shape even through the covering: the cocked angle of her neck, where her fingers dug into his hips, the crease of her knees.

From overhead, he heard more shuffling. Short, sharp breaths as his father and the photographer came clumsily down the stairs. They carried the body of Henry's mother into the sitting room, his father holding her up by her under-arms. They laid her across the chesterfield with a flop that shook down her spine, quivered through her legs. After a breath, they propped her into a sitting position just off-centre on the sofa.

Mr. Mitchell leaned over, panting, and waved his son over. "Come and sit now, Hal," he gasped. Henry didn't move. His father stepped over, took the boy by the hand, and led him to his place next to the sitting corpse. His father pushed him closer to his mother, so close that their hips almost touched, then took Henry's sweaty hand and wrapped it inside her cold, dead one, closing the fingers one by one.

Henry stared at his hand, wrapped in hers, and tried to convince his nerves that they were not being truthful. Her touch was not so cold that it burned. When he closed his eyes it got better and then when he reopened them every part of his hand that was in contact with hers ached. It was just in his head. He could hear the voices of his father and the other man nearby but the words were floating past him. His father snapped his fingers and touched him on the shoulder and Henry looked at something other than his hand.

"You've sat for a photograph before, then?" the man asked. "Just be still, like that last time."

"Her eyes don't look right," said Mr. Mitchell. He came closer, bringing his face within inches of the body. Henry looked from his father to his mother. Her eyes were horrible and somehow his father looked right into them.

"Easily mended," said the other man. He took up a tiny bottle from among his things. Under the top was a tiny paintbrush that reached into the vial. Henry smelled a bitter chemical as the photographer painted a thin line under Mrs. Mitchell's eyebrow and another along her eyelashes and thumbed the lid upward, holding it there for a few seconds. Then he did the same to the other eye.

The man stood behind the camera. "Mister Mitchell, stand behind there and point her head toward me please." He did. "Alright young man, look right into the camera. And be still."

Right away Henry felt the urge to move. Like it was the only thing that might keep him alive. He tensed and held rigid. Tried not to touch the inside of his dead mother's hand. She was horribly still. He remembered posing for the other photograph, how remarkably still she had been even then. The transmogrification he had felt beginning on him years before had managed to claim her instead.

He felt her grip tightening but he knew that was impossible. His nerves misfiring again. He stayed fixed on the camera but started to think that she was ever so slightly turning her head. Bringing her stuck-open eyes around to stare into his. He looked at the photographer, then his father. Surely they would be reacting if she were moving. Or maybe she was moving too slowly for them to notice. So imperceptibly that only Henry could tell. The smell of the glue grew worse and his muscles and joints were sore from the effort of holding still. Even if the opportunity should arise, he might not be able to move. He had become petrified. Just like her.

Then her head did turn. It lolled heavily towards Henry and the weight and momentum pulled her shoulders down into a slouch. The edge of her ribs eased into him, her shoulder seeming to come around so her arms could get around him. He shrieked and jumped off the sofa. His hand was still gripped in hers. He pulled hard, yanking his hand free and dragging her whole body off of the chesterfield.

Both Mr. Mitchell and the photographer shouted as they hurried to gather Mrs. Mitchell up out of the heap she had become on the floor. Her face was pressed into the carpet, the glued-open eyes staring forward even as they brushed the fibres. Henry stared, waiting for the eyes to dart around, to seek him out. But soon Mr. Mitchell and the other man had her propped back on the couch just as before, staring lazily forward. They could not manage to keep her from slumping to one side.

"One moment," the photographer said, shuffling through one of the cases he had not yet unpacked. "I'm terribly sorry, mister Mitchel, that I didn't think to use this straightaway. Lift her head and hold it just like that." He brought over what looked like a metal post. At the top was a joint then an arm that reached outward and ended in a clamp. The two prongs were rounded like the backs of spoons. After turning wing nuts to adjust the height and the angle of the protruding arm he set the prongs on either side of Mrs. Mitchell's head and then turned another wing nut to hold it all in place.

"Come on now, Hal," said Mr. Mitchell, frustration oozing from his face. Henry stood behind the camera and didn't move. "Now, Henry."

"He's been through a lot, just now," said the photographer. "I understand. At the same time, we have to start the exposure over again and we're losing light."

Mr. Mitchell took a breath. "You heard him, Henry." He took the boy by the shoulders and marched him to the chesterfield, sitting him down like before. Once again, he set Mrs. Mitchell's stiff hand around the boy's small fingers. Henry would not look at the camera. Instead, he turned hard to the side, looking straight at his mother's head, now clamped in place. He stayed motionless, put all his effort into willing her to keep still.

"Henry, we don't have time for this," his father said.

Henry did not respond.

"Damn it, boy," his father shouted.

Henry jumped a little at the noise but didn't turn his head. After a minute or so of quiet, the photographer spoke up. "You know, it doesn't look bad like that. Has a kind of reverence. It looks almost..."

"Spare me," started Mr. Mitchell.

"Devotional, I was going to say. Shall I carry on?"

"Yes, I suppose it will have to do," Mr. Mitchell said with a sigh.

After his mother's corpse was removed and buried, things improved slightly for Henry. There was a funeral which passed like a blur. He didn't know anyone who arrived, though the attendance was sparse. A few people approached Mr. Mitchell to offer condolences, which he mostly ignored, and the rest avoided having to speak to either him or Henry. Though it still came in fits and starts, Henry's ability to sleep did improve.

As the days went on, much of the daily business of the house fell to Henry as his father simply did not seem capable of doing anything useful. He sat on the edge of Mrs. Mitchell's bed, the dried and crumbling flower petals dropping around him, while Henry struggled to make simple meals like toast and jam or potatoes with pickled fish. He would clean the dishes and then started branching out to tidy other rooms. It's not even that his mother would normally do these things; there had been a maid who simply hadn't been present since he'd returned home.

Henry brought a waste basket from the kitchen up to his mother's bedroom. The stink of the dead flowers even reached downstairs and it was clear that alleviating that problem fell only to him. His father sat on the edge of the bed, as always. Silent. Not even looking around the room. Henry started with the flowers tied around pieces of the furniture, crushing them in his hands so they would take up less room in the basket. When he reached the bedposts, his father finally looked up. "What are you doing?"

"The flowers are all dead. They're stinking up the house," Henry said. He started gathering up all the petals placed around the bed, still in the approximate shape of his mother.

"You can't disturb this place, Henry. You've more sense that," said Mr. Mitchell, moving to stand. Henry continued on. Now that he had steeled up the nerve, he didn't want to lose it.

"Stop," his father cried, grabbing the boy's hands. His eyes were wild and red-rimmed, as though he had not slept. "This is your mother's room," he shouted.

"She isn't here," Henry stammered. "It's no one's," he whispered.

His father stared and then looked around the room. He said nothing more, just walked out. Henry stayed still a while, too afraid to move. He thought his mother would hate the mess if she saw it. She would also hate the idea of Henry touching her things, being in her space. She would have been unhappy no matter what, especially with her own death. Henry sighed, left the wastebasket on the bed and went back to his own room.

Henry didn't see his father at all the next day but the day after that he awoke to the sounds of many people moving about the main floor of the house, furniture being moved. He got out of bed and dressed quickly, making his way to the stairs. Before heading down, he noticed that his mother's room had been completely cleaned. There were no more flowers or candles or perfumes. The covers on the bed had been stripped. The window was open, the curtains removed. An empty ghost of a room.

He went downstairs and saw a few people milling about the sitting room. His father came into the hall. "Morning, Hal," he chirped. "There's breakfast in the kitchen. Just stay in there a while we finish clearing out the room here." Henry went into the kitchen where there was a still-steaming bowl of porridge next to a dish of honey. Right as he sat, his father popped in with the photograph of a much younger Henry sitting on a drape under which was his annoyed mother. Mr. Mitchell handed the frame to Henry. "Keep this safe in here," he said. Over the next hour or so, there was much noise from the sitting room but Henry did as he was bid and ate his breakfast, then waited at the table while the workmen removed the last of the furniture that his father had sold.

He heard the front door close and everything grow quiet but his father did not come back into the kitchen. After a few more minutes Henry pushed his chair back and went out to the sitting room. His father stood in the doorway, casting a dark silhouette. Past him, the room was bare. Only dirt on the floorboards and dust piled up in the corners remained. Mr. Mitchell breathed slowly, taking in the empty space.

"Is something wrong?" Henry asked.

Mr. Mitchell moved as if he'd been awoken from a nap. "Not at all. Just making sure they got everything," he said. He patted Henry on the shoulder. "Nothing for it now but to close it up."

He had Henry sweep out the room while he nailed boards over the room's two windows. He pounded the nails gingerly to avoid breaking the glass. "Fetch the lamp from the kitchen, would you," he said.

Working under lamplight, he and Henry measured out a length of thick canvas and covered the boarded windows. "This will keep the drafts out," Mr. Mitchell said. There was no longer any way for air or light to find their way in.

Henry and his father went out into the hall, bringing the lamp and closing the door tight behind them. Mr. Mitchell drove one nail at an angle through both the door and the frame. He tugged on the nailhead and, when it didn't budge, he gave the hammer to Henry. He showed the boy how to hold the nail in place and knock it just enough that it could stand on its own. "Now drive the bugger home," he said. "But make sure to leave it sticking out some. So that we'll be able to open it up again. Everything just as it was."

They covered the door with canvas much the same way as the windows. Mr. Mitchell took care of the nails at the top of the frame, leaving Henry to secure the rest. The boy felt rather practical and accomplished, as though he had completed a grownup task. He smiled at his father, who did smile in return but in a quiet way that reminded Henry that nothing about this day was to be celebrated.

"Listen, Hal. I'm sorry about the other day. Snapping at you. You were right that we do need to press on. It will be hard work to get everything back to normal." He began gathering up the tools. "I need to head back to work this afternoon. You'll be all right here by yourself," he stated, not asked.

"Yes, I suppose," Henry said.

"There's bread and jam in the pantry," Mr. Mitchell said as he went upstairs to change. Henry didn't feel much like eating anyway.

Over the next few days Henry and Mr. Mitchell established a pleasant if somewhat dull routine. Though Henry was alone quite a bit, he grew to enjoy the solitude and taught himself to do household tasks until his father returned in the evenings.

After everything became cozy and comfortable, the printed photograph of Henry and his dead mother arrived by post.

"Come have a look, Hal. You look like a proper gent," his father said, laying the stiff paper in his son's hands.

Henry couldn't look away from his mother, her eyes open so very wide. A dead stare. The detail was remarkable, every line and shape of her in sharp focus. Henry was clear enough but of course she had been more still than him. And though her gaze fell clumsily in the direction of the camera, Henry could feel her looking straight through the camera and into him.

"Bring it upstairs with you," his father said as he bounded up the steps. The picture emitted a chemical smell and Henry held the thing at arm's length, turning it to face away from him.

His father met him in his bedroom doorway with a small, wooden picture frame. "We only have the one but you can keep it in here," he said, smiling. He opened the back of the frame, took the photograph from Henry, and placed it inside. "You'll put it on your night table. She would have liked the idea of watching over you while you sleep." His father positively beamed.

"Don't you want to look at it," was all Henry managed to say.

"It's for you, Hal. I have many memories of your mother," he said, his eyes dampening. "You're still young and must never forget who your mother was." But Henry had nothing about her to forget. She remained a stranger, and now a dead stranger watching over his bed. "I'm glad it's you sat with her and not me. I'd have just uglied the thing up, I'm afraid."

Henry tried not to breathe too deep, his nostrils prickling at the smell of the glue.

"Is anything the matter, Hal?" Mr. Mitchell asked.

"I was just—" Henry paused, could just picture the expression on his dead mother's face souring at the nickname. "I was only looking at her," he said.

Mr. Mitchell patted the boy on the shoulder. He turned the boy's face up to his. "How about something hearty for supper tonight. Your colour is off. You could use some iron," he said as he headed downstairs.

Henry set the photograph down on the night table and shuffled out of the bedroom backwards, never taking his eyes off of it. He was sure it was about to do something awful.

As predicted, she did watch over him. That was the worst part. Henry was brought back to the few nights when his mother's body lay in the room down the hall but now she was only inches from his head. Try as he might, he could not keep his eyes closed. He had to watch, to make sure the picture hadn't moved. That she hadn't moved it. Despite the dark, he could still make out her stuck-open stare. After a few hours he spun the frame around so that it faced the wall.

Some time later he heard his father making his way to his own bed. Henry was still not asleep. Mr. Mitchell snuck a quick peek into his son's room and, seeing the photograph turned, stepped inside and spun it back around. His heavy slippers made a good deal of noise but Henry pretended to sleep through it. He stayed that way all night and in the morning he was quietly relieved to see that at least the photograph had not moved since his father had fussed with it. After that first night, Henry turned the photograph away every time he climbed into bed but every morning it was

188

spun back around to face him, even though he hadn't been roused by his father's heavy footfalls.

During the day, Henry welcomed as many distractions as possible. While his father returned to work and tended to business, Henry swept the staircase and the hallways. He dusted in the kitchen and his father's and mother's bedroom. Mrs. Mitchell's room remained an empty husk. It could have belonged to anyone or no one. It connected much more now with Henry's lack of memories of his mother than when she had lain in it. The one room he repeatedly neglected to clean and tidy was his own, because the photograph was in there. Once he was up and dressed, he would go all day without setting foot in that room.

Every week or so, Mr. Mitchell would leave behind a few coins and a short list of needed food items. These were Henry's favourite days and he could make a trip into town for bread and milk last a whole afternoon. Inevitably, though, he would have to return home, up to his room to bed, where the picture was always already waiting.

He began sneaking handkerchiefs from the top drawer of his father's dresser and, before sliding under the bedcovers, he'd spin the frame around and drape the cloth over it. But every morning the handkerchiefs were gone and the photograph looked at him from the edge of the night table.

Mr. Mitchell remarked that many of his handkerchiefs and some of the tea towels were missing so Henry had to stop pilfering them. It seemed that no matter what Henry tried he was going to wake up staring into his mother's dead eyes. It became terribly normal.

"What if we hung the picture over here?" Henry asked, holding the picture against the wall in the main hallway. "It looks nice in the light."

"Why did you bring it outside your room, Hal?" his father said as he came around from the kitchen. "Make sure to be careful if you're carrying that around." He looked quickly from the boy to the photograph. "I don't think that's a good place for it," he said.

Around a small corner at the foot of the stairs was a cherry-wood credenza where his father piled the mail. Henry set the frame on it and said, "It looks good over here."

"What's this then, Hal?" Mr. Mitchell said through a sigh. "It goes in your room so that your mother can watch over you."

"It's not right that I should have it all to myself," Henry said. "What about you?"

"That's very considerate, Hal, but it's meant to be something special for you. It's what your mother would want, don't you think?" Henry could not begin to imagine what it was his mother wanted. "Let's put it back in your room where it was," Mr. Mitchell said.

That night, Henry kept rousing from a light doze, unable to fall into normal sleep. It seemed exceptionally dark—he could make out the baseboards against the white walls. He could just make out the doorframe at the other end of the room. And the photograph facing him, pushed all the way to the edge of the night table.

Turning it away obviously did not work. Henry grabbed hold of the wretched thing and got out of bed. He slunk through the hall and down the steps to the front door. With tiny, minute movements, he turned the knob and felt a soft click as the latch came open.

He stood in the open doorway, though he couldn't see much of the street in the dark. Could it be as easy as tossing the photograph out? What would he say to his father? What plausible scenario could there be, other than Henry had thrown it away?

It was too dark to see past the front step but he could still see his mother's eyes. Peering at him. Assuring him of one thing: he would never be rid of her.

He closed the door and set the frame down on the credenza. He went upstairs to lie in bed awake for the few hours left until morning.

His father was making breakfast when Henry awoke. The photograph was once again on the night table, so close to the edge it threatened to topple down onto his head. Without even thinking he grabbed the thing and, with a shriek, flung it hard against the farthest wall. The glass cracked and the frame broke apart at the corners as it hit the floor. His father bounded up the stairs.

"What's happened?" he said.

Henry stayed in bed, half under the covers. Not answering.

"What have you done?" his father demanded, looking at the pieces on the floor. He stepped closer to the wreckage, glass crunching under his slippers. "Why do I have to keep putting up with this? You've no respect." He stooped and carefully lifted the photograph out, minding not to tear or scratch it. He left the room.

Henry breathed a great sigh. Perhaps his father would not trust him with the photograph anymore. That would be worth a lashing. He took the broom from the hall closet and began to clear up the mess he'd made.

After a few minutes, his father came back with the bare photograph pressed to his chest. He pulled aside the covers and sat, tugging Henry down beside him.

"Henry," he said. He was choosing his words carefully. "I know this return home has been dreadful. Everything turned on its head, having to leave your school, not to mention losing your mother so young. It's not the life I pictured for you. And this is no substitute for your mother being here." He thumbed the corner of the photograph and Henry looked at the blank side, hoping his father wouldn't turn it around. "But you must try to be grateful that we have it. It's more than a piece of paper, don't you see?"

Henry blinked.

"It's one of the few fortunes left to us," his father went on. "I will have everything set right, things will go back to normal. But until then, this is our reminder." He took the picture from his chest, laid it in his lap, and pulled Henry closer. "Your mother, in this picture," he said, "she looks just as I remember her." He kissed the boy on the head. "Get dressed and come down for breakfast," he said.

Henry dressed slowly, waiting for his father to leave for his own business. Eventually, he heard the door open and close. Only then did Henry go downstairs. In the kitchen he found bread and jam and an apple. His father had only cooked for himself.

On the table sat the photograph. The corners of the frame were pressed back together, no longer any glass in it. A hint of a chemical smell cut through the kitchen air. Henry opened one of the highest cupboards, cleared some space, and gingerly placed the frame face down inside. He closed the cupboard quietly, hoping the picture wouldn't realize he'd hidden it in there. On the counter were a few coins and a short list of sundries, both of which he pocketed. He took the bread and the apple with him and ate alone in his room.

Henry let himself into the house and brought his small bundle of goods into the kitchen. From the front door he walked down the hallway, past the sealed doors of the library and the dining room, and into the kitchen where he saw the pile of breakfast dishes he'd left out.

On the edge of the counter, in its new customary place since the sitting room had been sealed, sat the older photograph of him on his covered-over mother. It had been a long time since he'd even thought of it. Henry was a little surprised with himself that he didn't feel the same dread as he did for the new image.

He remembered how it had felt to hold so still when he was so little. He looked at the details of the room captured in the picture and realized that they were all gone: the armchair he and his mother sat on had been sold, the clothes he wore were now far too small, the sitting room where he'd posed was closed off, and of course his mother was dead. Everything was moving forward without him, while his father held to the idea of a return to normal.

Henry could see the shape of one of his mother's hands through the heavy drape, clenched tightly around his hip. It was easy to make out her posture. The shape of her under the fabric was familiar, her head tilted to one side.

He could even make out the intricate pattern of the drape itself. He remembered that the cloth had been yellow, though he hadn't seen it since. It was a horrid, ugly pattern. Arabesque was the word for it, he thought. It was made of shapes that drooped and lolled and curved without seeming to repeat. He chose one point and tried to follow the pattern to an end, tracing his eyes along the lines, over folds and creases, looking for it to come back over itself. The detail was remarkably clear, he thought. How still his mother must have stayed that whole time. He followed the pattern up to the spot where the fabric was laid over her head. Here the shapes became decidedly round and bulbous. He stared at two prominent orbs in the deepest part of the cloth and after a long quiet moment, they blinked open. His mother's dead frozen eyes. They

193

stared at him through the pattern. Through the photograph. Right through him.

Henry ran from the kitchen. He didn't scream. He flew up the stairs, straight to his bedroom. He stopped cold when he saw the photograph on his night table. The broken frame around the picture of him and his dead mother. In its customary place. Not in the cupboard where he'd left it.

There was nowhere to go. He went for his father's tools and came back with a hammer and one long nail. He went right to the photograph, half expecting it to jump out at him or rush from his grasp. He pushed the face of the frame flat against the wall and jammed the nail into the back. Once it was deep enough to stay on its own, he swung the hammer with both hands. He stopped when the head of the nail was flush against the back of the frame.

He paced up and down the hallway, poking his head into the room to make sure the thing was still nailed in place. Eventually he felt safe enough to move about the house. Downstairs, he boiled water for tea. He had a generous helping of bread and jam, eating until he was full. For a fleeting moment, he felt as though he had accomplished something grown-up and worthwhile. Then worries about his father's reaction crept into his thoughts.

It was moments away from sunset. Mr. Mitchell was later than usual. If he was late enough, Henry could already be in bed when his father got home. If the bedroom door were closed, he would surely let the boy sleep and then there wouldn't be an opportunity to see the photograph until morning.

Henry returned to his room, elated that the picture was still nailed to the wall. Facing away. Just as he'd left it. He sat on his bed and waited for his father to come home. For a short while there was enough light by which to read but he found it hard to concentrate. He didn't get up, not even to pull the curtains or light the lamps. He just let it get dark. The photograph stayed stuck to the wall, shadows creeping in a slow circle around the frame until all was black.

After some time, he heard the sound of keys and footsteps. Quickly but without hurrying Henry closed the door to his room, climbed under the covers, and pretended to be asleep.

Mr. Mitchell was not quiet as he came into the house but he didn't call out. Henry heard his footsteps as checked the kitchen then trudged up the stairs. The door handle clicked when his father turned and opened it just wide enough to step inside. Henry fought a desperate compulsion to move. His father kept standing there.

The floorboards creaked as he rocked his weight between his heels and the balls of his feet. Henry held his breath. His father let out a great long sigh that sounded rather sad. He lingered a moment then softly left the room. He made almost no noise at all.

Henry took a relieved gasp of air. The room felt safe and warm, which it hadn't for a long while. The sound of his father moving about in other parts of the house was comforting. And though Henry was accustomed to lying in bed awake most of the night, this time he fell asleep.

When Henry awoke in the morning, his mother's dead eyes were the first sight to greet him. The photograph was once again in its customary place on the night table. A hole punched through it. Near the top. The long nail lying next to the frame.

He didn't throw the picture or even reach out to touch it. He recoiled. Henry scrambled away until his back was against the wall. He turned away. Clamped his eyes shut. He wriggled as deep into the corner between the bed and the wall as he could. The smooth plaster was cold on his nose and forehead.

But his eyelids wouldn't stay shut. He used all his effort, all his will, to hold them closed. He felt his eyelids peeled upward and then held open. Still he could feel the plaster of the wall against his face but he did not see the wall. He was inside the sitting room, on the chesterfield. The heavy woven yellow rug was under his feet.

He could not move but he did feel his itchy clothes. The lumpy sofa cushions, the snugness of his shoes. One of his hands was held by something cold. He caught a chemical taint in the air. The smell of glue. The thing clamped on his hand squeezed tighter. It started to hurt. Henry could only move his head and, even then, only in one direction. His dead mother sat beside him, her dead hand clamped around his. Her head turned. Ever so slightly. Her neck lolled, her face drooped down towards Henry. He fought in vain to look away. Her enormous stuck-open eyes grabbed onto his with tremendous force and in a slow, draining blink, the only thing left in all the world for him to do was to stare back at her forever.

More often than not, the classic ghost story is basically a murder mystery. The haunting is an attempt to communicate what happened to the person who became a ghost: how they died, who killed them. If the person being haunted can solve the mystery, they are rewarded by then being free of the ghost. And comeuppance only comes to the killer once their misdeeds are exposed.

Many American (and some Canadian) ghost stories rely on the tired trope of the "Indian burial ground." But this is rooted in the same basic ghost story structure. The colonizers are the evildoers and they could be subject to retribution at any time. This scares the hell out of most middle-class white people: that one day their complicity or simply the fact that they enjoy the aftereffects of a historical genocide, might be used to judge them.

Like the final girl, there is a modern twist on this ghost story structure that subverts this expectation. It can be seen in novels such as *The Woman in Black* by Susan Hill and *Ring* by Koji Suzuki. In these stories, there remains the mystery of who the ghost is and what happened to them. But uncovering the truth does not "cure" the ghost. It remains and it continues to haunt and, in these two cases, continues to kill victims. There is no appeasing the ghost. It cannot be stopped.

It never stops

GIZZARD STONES

The basic experiment is pretty simple," the professor said. Casey had been to two meetings already but none had yet detailed the specifics. This time they did not meet in the psychology department, as they normally did, but in the robotics lab. "Casey, can you take this spot here in the middle?" the professor asked, stepping forward. She wore bold, thick-rimmed red glasses. Casey wasn't sure why, but she had expected her to be wearing a lab coat.

Casey sat on a high stool, unable to touch the ground, though there was a bar where she could rest her feet. She was in the centre of a long row of identical stools with identical setups. In front of her, and in front of every other seat, was a small flat panel with only a red plastic button in easy reach. The apparatus behind each stool was more elaborate, starting with a thick rope of wires that ran from underneath the red button panel, through the legs and under the stool, linking a mechanical rig with a robotic arm protruding out of a maze of gears and other moving parts. The arm itself had one joint in the middle like an elbow that bent towards Casey. At the end of the arm there was a rubber-capped digit, about the size of two fingers.

"The red button in front here controls the arm apparatus behind you," the professor said as she moved down the row, gesturing for the other participants to take their spots as Casey had. "All the talk yesterday of ghosts seemed to leave everyone confused, so I'll spell it out." Casey noticed that she was grinding her teeth, or rather she noticed that the other participants kept looking in her direction trying to figure out where that click-scrape sound was coming from. Now she, too, heard the sound of her teeth scraping against each other like stones. She popped a piece of gum in her mouth. Chewing was essentially the same motion, but quieter.

"The concept we'll be testing here borrows a little from psychology but also veers into neuroscience, some theoretical physics, and all facilitated by the engineering and robotics department, who have set us up with these," she gestured at the arms, moving back down the row.

The professor came right to Casey. "May I?" Casey nodded, not yet sure for what she was giving permission. The professor stepped closer, squared Casey's shoulders so that her back was fully turned to the machine arm, pushed in her low back so she sat up straight. "Each time you push the button, the robot arm will respond by gently touching your back."

The professor pushed Casey's button and the arm did indeed extend a few inches and poked Casey in the middle of her back.

"For the first while, the arm will respond right away, in the exact same time interval, every time that button is pressed."

The professor pushed the button again and, again, Casey felt the gentle poke at her back. "But as the experiment goes on, the AI controlling the arm will start to randomly adjust the response interval. There may be a long delay before the arm actually pokes you, or it may seem to respond impossibly fast, as though you haven't even finished pushing the button. But it can only respond if you push it and it will respond to every button press. You just won't be able to predict exactly when.

"Is everyone familiar with proprioception? Oversimplified, this is the brain's perception of the position of the body, and what's around it, in physical space. An example would be if you've ever misjudged the number of stairs. Oddly disorienting. Or reaching for something in the dark and misjudging where you or the object actually are. It's an eerie feeling. It's a minor miscalculation but as a matter of consciousness—in a cosmic sense, to blow it way out of proportion—it's essentially a realization that you are not in fact where you thought you were. In those few seconds it takes for your brain to readjust, correct its perception, you are left with the dread of what else you might have missed," the professor said. She was growing more animated even as the class was deflating.

"The randomized interval of the robot is meant to trigger this exact feeling. After long enough, the inability to predict the robot's response will affect your perception of the surrounding environment."

She grinned, enjoying this part. "It will probably begin to feel like it's not you in control but a separate entity. It may even get to the point that you feel it is not the robot arm poking you but something else. Some*one* else." She shivered.

"Consciously, you will know that's not the case. Everyone will be able to see everyone else. I'll be asking lots of questions throughout the experiment and you'll be able to hear everyone else's answers. You'll be able to see the whole space throughout the experiment and so you'll be able to see that there are no other entities or figures here in the room with us. You will consciously understand the circumstances of the delay and that the robot is only responding to your button pushes. But it won't feel that way," she said.

"The purpose of this experiment is to create, within a clinical and reproducible setting, the emotional experience of a haunting."

When Casey was little, she'd had pica. Still had it, she supposed, but she'd managed to go so long without an incident that she considered the disorder well and truly dealt with. Most of the episodes that had worried her family so—the most troublesome ones—Casey did not remember firsthand. She remembered having pica and what it was. She knew that she had compulsions that were abnormal, certain impulses she needed to hide or she'd face correction. But the many visits to the emergency room her family brought up every so often, she didn't fully recollect.

She did remember them in that peculiar kind of constructed way, her mind assembling the framework of memories after hearing the same stories over and over. Whole parts of Casey's childhood were really cobbled together from pieces of everyone else's memories.

She'd never eaten metal or glass, which was apparently quite a relief. Occasionally she'd eaten dirt or sand, always in such ready supply around small children. She'd been fond of chalk which would give her terrible cramps as it ground its way out of her system. But most of all she was drawn to eating tiny stones. Small pebbles, sometimes gravel, though she preferred smooth edges. She liked the idea of them collecting in her belly, click-clacking against each other when she moved. The sounds they made against her teeth gave her goosebumps.

Her parents scolded her of course. At first, they thought she was just clicking her teeth together. As Casey's habit got worse, her parents constantly demanded to look inside her mouth. She got pretty good at swallowing the precious stones before probing adult fingers could pry them from her jaws. She did remember very clearly that if she ever picked anything up off the ground in sight of her parents, they would quickly smack it out of her hands.

When Casey was eight, she discovered in an encyclopedia in the school library that certain types of birds eat small round stones and store them in their bellies to break down the food they can't chew because, of course, birds have no teeth. This made perfect sense to her and little-girl Casey reasoned that she must be part bird herself. That would explain a great many things and she tried in vain to convince her family of this fact. Every time they refused to believe her, she assured them that they were going to look very foolish indeed when her other bird qualities started to come in.

That same year, she chipped three of her newly-adult teeth chewing on rocks and other inedibles: two on the top, one on the bottom. The total would eventually rise to twelve of her permanent teeth that were jagged and broken or, as in two extreme cases, pulled almost as soon as they came in. Her parents were not able to pay to cap the teeth that were damaged. They had spent all of their money on Casey's therapist, they liked to remind her, though years later they would insist that had been a joke. Besides, they'd continue, her little snaggle-toothed grin was really very cute.

Once Casey was old enough to start thinking about moving away to university, her parents began to worry about how they could possibly be expected to pay for it. They pestered her about scholarships or whether she was even sure that she wanted to continue past high school. Maybe she could just work a year or two first, give them more time to come up with a plan. So Casey offered them a deal: she would pay for school herself, no contributions from mom or dad needed, but they would have to come up with a way to pay for her teeth. Her parents were split up by this time, so they would have to work together to come up with that much, though it would surely be less than years of school. They agreed and, after several procedures, Casey's teeth were capped. The work was impeccable. Her parents still looked at her as their daughter, of course, but their little-girl Casey was fully replaced in just about a blink; her new perfect smile turning her into an instant adult, exacerbating those problems all parents face when their children grow up. It was hard for them.

Casey, on the other hand, could not have been more pleased.

Her own history undoubtedly played some part in Casey's interest in psychology. She remembered the first time she looked up "pica" herself. For a long time it was considered a disorder rooted in greed. Just an insatiable maw stuffing in everything at hand. But like most things, the reality is more complicated and less logical. It gave Casey some comfort to know that pica was now understood as much more closely related to anxiety. This gave her something to work with and a way of understanding the ebb and flow of her compulsion. For sometimes it was worse and she was more conscious of stifling the desire to eat the little gizzard stones. Understanding was just about the only power she had over it.

The first day of the experiment was a Friday, but apparently the weekend break between the explanatory lecture and the action phase was important.

"How many of you have seen a ghost?" the professor asked. She held out for the long silence, making eye contact with each student. "It's not a trick question. It even plays into the study, but perhaps not as directly as you might think. I'll ask again, has anyone here ever seen a ghost?" Still nothing.

"If any of you are familiar with my research, you will have noticed that I have a soft spot for the supernatural. As it pertains to psychology, of course. The supernatural is an inextricable component of the human psyche and I am particularly interested in the concept of the ghost and what it can tell us about general human psychology." She paced in front of the row of students.

"The idea of the ghost exists in virtually every culture and mythology in the world. There are variations but there is always some form in which the spirit or consciousness of those who have died linger in a way that can be perceived, even if only barely, by the living. In some cultures, this is wholly benevolent—the loving guidance of ancestors steering us through our lives. In others, the ghost is threatening and dangerous. Then there is every possible iteration or combination in between.

"Allow me to try a slightly different tack: who here believes in ghosts?" The participants looked one to another, making nervous eye contact. One hand went up. Then another. "Excellent," the professor said. "As is now clear, this opinion is not evenly distributed among you. This is good, helps us avoid obvious bias. In fact, whether you consider yourself a believer or not, the details of your belief, the nuances, are likely to be wildly different than anyone else's, even someone who shares the same ultimate belief.

"Given that every culture throughout human history has had some concept that could be considered a version of a ghost, it's odd then that a ghost is something that most people will tell you does not exist. Science denies ghosts. But stories and belief in them persists.

"There is no proof that ghosts exist, nor is there proof that they do not. There is an additional complication. Almost every famous haunting or sighting or bit of evidence that purports to be true proof of a haunting has eventually been revealed to be false. Not just mistaken or incorrect, but hoaxes. Outright lies. But this doesn't really sway anyone. The belief, the faith in the ghost, wins out."

Casey's family had a small cottage when she was young. It was sold as part of her parent's divorce well before she moved away to school, but she remembered it vividly. The most prominent memory was a dark one, though her family maintained that she had made something out of nothing. To this day, it would seem, there was still no recognition of the fact that she had been right.

Though it would remain a core memory, Casey struggled to remember her exact age when it happened. She was definitely a teenager though she was still too young to drive. Somewhere in the maelstrom of the teenage upheaval.

She and her father had driven up to the cottage, just the two of them, to close the place up for the winter. On the long drive, her father rattled off a few of the things that would need to be done, asking her to remind him if they forgot any before they went home. It would be good to clean up the yard before the snow came, get all the fallen branches, cut the grass. Lock up the shed. Turn off the water, clear out the pipes and toilet. Check the windows.

The cottage was well back from the road, an overgrown path of paving stones leading right up to the door. It was two storeys, kind of. Two small bedrooms on the upper floor, inches away from the roof. Casey knew it was probably supposed to be an attic but her dad had put up walls and two doors, making two tiny bedroom spaces and a narrow hallway.

As they pulled up, Casey saw someone standing in the window. Her bedroom window. Looking down at them.

"There's someone in there," she said and pointed. When her father didn't respond, she grabbed his arm. "There's someone inside," she said louder. When she turned back to the cottage, the window was empty.

"I didn't see anyone," he said. Her father was sure no one was inside but promised that he would check. The front door was locked, the whole area so quiet. No one around here would break in.

He checked all the downstairs first, the kitchen, pantry, bathroom, the little mudroom at the back porch, despite Casey's insistence that someone was upstairs. Everything looked in order, she admitted, but it all felt wrong. The cottage didn't feel empty.

"Let's go upstairs then," her father said.

Casey held her breath as they went up. She tried to listen for sounds of someone moving around but her father's footsteps were so heavy, the stairs creaked and groaned and drowned out all the smaller sounds she might have detected. Both bedroom doors were open, the floor needing to be swept. Her dad poked his head into both rooms, then turned to her. "See? Both empty. No one's here."

"The closet," Casey said. Her room had a small closet space, right where the slope of the roof met the wall her father had put up. Not really a closet. It wasn't contained either, but rather a small space that ran between the wall and the edge of the roof, like a crawl space that circled the second floor. It let in a cool draft from outside. She'd always found it spooky. Her father opened the closet door. It was dark, that same familiar draft. Neither saw anyone but her father didn't look as though he wanted to crawl around behind the wall.

"Still no one," he said. "Come on. There's lots to do." He shooed her back down the stairs and gave her a garbage bag to clean out the fridge and the pantry while he crawled under the sink to turn the water off. Then he went outside to deal with the yard and left her to keep cleaning.

Inside the cottage, by herself, every creak sounded like someone upstairs trying desperately not to be seen. Casey stood at the base of the stairs for a long time, looking up, too scared to go back into the upper rooms to look on her own. She never did see anyone the rest of that day, but she felt them. She knew someone was there.

"You're being silly," her father said as they drove home.

The room was filled with nervous giggles, little gasps, as everyone all down the row kept getting poked in the back by the mechanical arms. "Be sure to take notes about any changes in your feelings. Look around to everyone else, feel free to ask your neighbours how they are feeling too," the professor said. "The feedback from others is part of the experiment. If the haunted feeling still emerges despite distractions, then that speaks well to the experiment's repeatability," she went on, moving down the line, smiling, trying not to giggle herself.

Casey pushed the button and the robot finger poked. It was still quite gentle, the timing predictable. She was extra aware of the exact spot where it touched. It was always the same and she started to wonder if she might develop a bruise, even though the contact was so light. Her jaw was getting sore. She had swallowed her gum and found herself biting down hard to keep from grinding her teeth.

"Leaving aside the question of whether or not ghosts do

tangibly exist, which isn't the actual focus of this experiment, what about the *experience* of them? Something that stands out to me is the bridging quality. Ghosts are a connection between the living and the dead. What do we say when someone dies? They have *passed*, they are in *a better place*, they have *ascended*. There is a pervasive sense of death being a journey to a destination. A ghost has either made that journey and come back, or has gotten lost along the way.

"Why are ghosts explained this way? In terms of psychological meaning, why have folklore and mythology adopted these qualities for ghosts and the dead? From a psychological and sociological point of view, folklore is attempting to provide explanations for things that we cannot explain. Giving a reason to things we don't understand. There is so much we don't understand about death."

Casey pushed the button. Waited.

"What can we say about being alive?" the professor asked.

Casey yelped as she was poked, the longest interval yet. It had surprised her, despite knowing it would come eventually. The professor was distracting her. She pushed the button again.

The professor went on. "Anything we do say about being alive, positive or negative, is filtered through our minds against the opposite. So the hidden subtext of that question is really a veiled attempt to contemplate the opposite: what can we say about being dead? A concept that our minds can not comprehend. The brain can not understand what it is to not exist.

"Psychology, philosophy, science, can not tell us what it is like to be dead. So religion and mythology try to fill that void for us. But mythological concepts of death all resemble a kind of life. Death cannot be nothing, because we can't understand that. But if death were like life—an afterlife, per se—that we could comprehend. What if being dead was just like being alive?"

It was something her therapist said early on that got through to Casey. She was young at this point, still a little girl, coming to terms with the fact that she was probably not part bird and that no other bird-like qualities were on the way. Her pica was simmering but under control. She mostly snuck small pinches of dirt when no one was looking. If things were especially bad, she would snatch a pebble off the ground and hold it in her mouth, swallowing as soon as someone noticed. She had become expert at reacting when people asked, "What's in your mouth," able to swallow and say "nothing" simultaneously. This was much better than it had been.

After a few sessions, the therapist asked Casey if she might have a look at her teeth. In reflex, Casey pulled her lips tight over her mouth. "I know that it's uncomfortable for you," the therapist said, "but I think it will help to gradually think about them less. We've been talking for quite a while now. I've seen them. This isn't about my curiosity. The point is for me to look at your teeth when you know that I am looking at them. Can we give it a try?"

Casey bit at her lips a little before making a simian tooth-baring smile.

"No need to smile," the therapist responded. "We're not taking a picture. Just show them off. Let them stick out." Casey did. She opened her mouth, pulled her lips back. She had gotten so used to unconsciously resting her lips as far over her teeth as she could that it felt odd to let the cold air touch them.

"I know these are your adult teeth and that it feels like you're stuck with them forever. But I want you to think about what makes you *you*. What makes Casey *Casey*? Because it isn't your teeth. We're constantly changing who we are. We don't stay the same for very long. Even physical bodies change entirely. You're old enough to know that our bodies are made up of cells. You've talked about that in science class? We're made up of trillions upon trillions of tiny, microscopic cells but no one cell defines who we are. Somehow all of those cells taken together do make us into something.

"And cells, just like anything else alive, die and are replaced. Our bodies are constantly losing cells but also constantly replacing them. This process takes about seven years for every cell in your body to be replaced. So in a way, every seven years, we are in a completely different physical body than we were seven years before. And our minds and our personalities can change like that as well. In that way, we can also change, knowing that we are constantly renewing, changing, growing. Those may be your permanent teeth, Casey. But who you are right now, in this moment, does not need to be permanent. You can shed and leave behind parts of you that you don't like. Bring in those new cells. And before you know it, even on a cellular level, this version of Casey that is hurting will be all the way gone."

"I'm glad you agreed to come with me again," her father said. "It's important that we do stuff, just the two of us. I know this is a bit of a chore but it'll make you appreciate every other visit later in the year." He said this only after a more than two-hour drive in near total silence. They had only stopped briefly at the grocery store in town for cleaning supplies and sandwiches for lunch. They weren't even going to spend the night; after who knew how many hours of cleaning, Casey and her father would spend another awkward two and a half hours driving home. "Let's do a lap first, see if any trees came down over the winter."

Casey didn't want to get out of the car. It was cold, the earth still frozen and mostly covered in snow. The ground crunched with ice under her boots. Her mother had complained over and over that it was too early to open up the cottage for the season but the first trip out was her father's favourite. Years later, Casey's therapist would help her understand that her father enjoyed being out there alone and she would regret not realizing that he was trying to share this private enjoyment with her.

There were a few larger branches littering the ground but no trees had come down, which was lucky. Her father talked nonstop as they trudged over the frozen slush, out of breath but still telling her how much it had cost to have the municipality send over someone to cut up the big oak that had fallen a few years back. One time, he'd found a dead deer near the beach, right where the sand gave way to grass. Despite repeated calls, it had stayed there over two weeks. Once it was gone, her father chuckled that he did not really want to know the specifics. His friend in town, who lived there year-round, was sure that the town hadn't come for it. Just reclaimed by the wilderness, he thought.

"Right around there," he said, pointing. The grass and bushes were so high Casey wouldn't have been able to see a deer standing to its full height in that spot. "Listen to the waves," her father said with a deep sigh.

Casey shivered and wiped the moisture building under her nostrils. "Can we go inside please?"

"It's not going to be much warmer in there, kiddo. No heat. But once we get going, you'll work up a sweat and won't even notice the cold." He took a few more breaths, just relishing the empty beach, the quiet, the cold, the dark gray sky overhead. "Alright, fun part's over."

Casey groaned.

They made their way back to the little cottage, retracing their steps where the path would have been, if anyone had been around to clear it. Casey went back to the car first, grabbed the bag of supplies, and turned her focus to following her footsteps in a path to the front door. Her father got a small shovel out of the trunk.

"The key is under the third stone from the steps. Sometimes it takes me a few tries to find the path," he said. He plunged the plastic blade a few times, not reaching the ground. Maybe just a hint of grass below.

"Why don't you just keep the keys with your house keys?" Casey asked.

"Because if we ever got all the way out here and I had forgotten them, or your mother came on her own, you'd have to drive all the way back to the city. No one but us knows they're there. Should have brought another shovel," he muttered.

Bored and cold, Casey trudged up to the porch and tried the front door. It was indeed locked. She sighed with exasperation. "Da-ad," she said.

"I'm working on it. We'll be inside in a minute. Walk around and brush the snow off the windowsills. Don't want snow falling in when we open them. Bad for the wood." The shovel cut through the ice and thudded against stone underneath. "Ha," he said.

Casey kicked some snow off the steps. She tucked her hand inside her coat sleeve and pushed all the snow off the sill of the window that looked into the kitchen. She peered in, saw the small table with four chairs around it. The table should have been clear, just dust-covered, but it was strewn with garbage. A lot of tiny crab apple cores but also water bottles, chip bags, cracker boxes.

"Dad," she said. He just kept digging. Maybe he didn't hear her. Had she said it loud enough? Near the edge of the table, right where the living/dining room led to the staircase, she saw boots laid on the ground. Not just boots. Pants. Legs. A coat. A person laying on the floor, legs toward the window Casey was looking through. The person's head was on the ground near the foot of the stairs.

"There's someone inside," she said.

The shovel crunched through snow.

"*Dad*. Stop."

"I can't let you in without the key, Casey. You want me to break the door down?" he said without looking up.

"There's a person inside the cottage," she said as she jumped off the porch towards him. This time he looked up. "There's someone in there already."

Her father dropped the shovel and came up to the porch with her. Casey moved back to the kitchen window and pointed but her father got a better view through the glass inlay on the door. She couldn't believe she hadn't noticed when she'd tried the knob.

"Oh, shit," her father said, trying the handle. He crashed his shoulder against the door and the whole cottage shook but the door held tight.

"Hello?" he called. "Can you hear me? Hello!" He ran back to the slightly uncovered path and grabbed the shovel. "Help me get the key," he said.

Casey remained frozen, looking through the window at the person on the floor inside the cottage. Her father had seen it too. There really was a person inside the cottage.

"Casey!"

She spun and looked at her father who was scrambling

to clear the snow away. "Third paving stone," he said, out of breath. Casey stepped off the porch and her father slung loads of snow in the air, hitting her in the face.

"Dad, Jesus."

"You're not helping," he said.

"What do you want me to do? There's only one shovel." He dug faster but was only moving the snow around, more of it falling back onto the path than he had managed to clear.

"Slow down," Casey said. She heard the plastic shovel crack against the frozen ground. "*Dad, stop!*" she yelled. He finally did, stood straight, monstrously out of breath. Huge gouts of steam poured from his mouth. Casey reached over and grabbed the shovel from him. "I'll find it," she said. "Call for help. Try the windows."

Her father pulled his phone out of his pocket and looked to her again, eyes wide with worry.

"I got this," she said.

He took huge steps, working around to the back of the cottage while looking at his phone screen. He banged on the walls of the cottage with the other hand, moving from window to window, calling to the person inside.

After a few minutes, he came back around. "There's no fucking bars out here. Not even 911 works. The windows are all frozen shut but the one at the back is slanted a little in the frame. Won't budge now but that must be how they got in," he said.

Casey had cleared the path to the third stone and was struggling to get the edge of the shovel underneath it, create enough leverage to lift it out of the ground. "Okay, here we go," her father said, crouching down. As soon as Casey got the stone high enough for him to get his fingers under, he pushed her aside, flipped the stone over into the snow, the key gleaming against the dirt. He had the door open and was inside before Casey had even dropped the shovel.

The inside of the cottage smelled off. There was an under-pinning of garbage and rot but the cold dulled the sting so it was pervasive but not overpowering. The unpleasant sweet-ness of browned apples hung heavy, as did a particular foulness Casey couldn't place. Something she'd not encountered before. Her father was on the ground beside the person, the body, and had flipped them onto their back. They were smaller than Casey's father, probably about Casey's size but it was hard to tell without laying down right beside them, which she would not. Casey could see the face now but it was shrunken and dry like a mummy. The eyes were closed, the mouth open. The teeth looked too big for the head but that was because the lips and cheeks had pulled so far back, the skin had shriveled away.

It looked to Casey as though it was a woman. Her father shook her by the shoulders, took his glove off and felt at the neck, under the chin. There was no way this person was alive but her father didn't seem ready to accept that conclusion.

"I don't think you should be touching her," Casey said. Her father looked up, confused. "Evidence or something. She's dead, Dad. We need to get an ambulance. Or the police." Her father sat back on his heels. He pulled his phone out of his pocket, showed her the no signal error. Casey checked hers to the same result.

"I'll have to drive into town. Or find someone with a land-line." He looked around. "What are you going to do?" he asked.

"I'm not staying here!" Casey said. "We'll both go. You drive and I'll try to get a signal." They stood. Casey held her father's elbow, led him out the door. She pulled the door shut.

"Did you lock it?" he asked.

"It's fine," she said.

No one had visited her since she moved away for school. It was liberating, especially at first, to not worry about check-ins, about what someone might infer from the placement of her dirty clothes, the state of her desk, the greasiness of her hair. But she had been on her own a long time now, left to deal with her stresses without an outlet, no therapist unless she wanted to use the student union's volunteer counselors and she didn't trust them. Coming up with the money to get here had been doable but now that she was here, having enough time for her schoolwork and to put together enough money to stay in the minimum number of classes to qualify for her dorm room was a grind. She was relieved to be advanced enough in the program to qualify to participate in these studies, because they paid. But none had chosen her as a subject until this one with the ghost machine. The money was welcome, but it wouldn't stretch far.

Not long before the study was to begin, after she knew that she had been chosen as a participant, Casey began to see her room as an outsider might. The tiny room was disorganized and cluttered, not how she preferred to live at home. There were clothes on the floor, books in piles and stacks that had fallen over on the ground. The small rug she'd bought to cover the freezing concrete floor was bunched up in a heap. When she'd first arrived on campus, she managed to convince the registrar to let her live alone, a luxury normally only afforded to graduate and PhD students. She'd dropped small hints about her history with a mental illness and the lack of qualified counseling here on campus. She intimated that the stress of living with a new person might prove too much for her. But what had she done with that privacy?

The only food in the room was a few packages of ramen noodles. She had an electric kettle. Many other students had a hot plate, even though they weren't allowed. For the first long while, she had kept fruits and vegetables in the mini fridge, something with nutritional value she could snack on.

She realized that she had not yet eaten at all today, couldn't remember when she had last had a real meal rather than just snacks from a vending machine. Her mouth was dry, thirsty.

She popped a piece of gum in her mouth and started to tidy the place up. She picked all the books up off the floor, set them neatly on her desk. She shook the rug out into the hallway and swept the whole room before replacing it. Standing in the middle of the room, having accomplished just this little bit, she felt better, more composed. She chewed faster.

She made her bed, pulling the blankets tight and straight, folding the top three inches of the sheet over the comforter. She put her dirty clothes in her already-heavy laundry bag. She'd do a wash tomorrow. She sniffed at the shirt she was wearing, pushing her nose into her armpits. These clothes needed to be washed, too. But her closet, the lone rod with a shelf above it built into the wall, was bare. She had one pair of dress pants that were clean, still in a dry-cleaning bag because she hadn't worn them even once since arriving. Everything else was dirty. She upended the laundry bag, looking for something that was in better shape that she could wear to do the laundry now. How much was left in her account? The experiment wouldn't pay for a couple weeks yet. She could sell off some of her textbooks, get them from the library instead.

She had that eerie feeling, as though someone was in the room watching her. If she'd had a roommate she could ask, "What are you looking at?" They would answer her. There wouldn't be this silence, this foreboding absence. The quiet carried with it an implied threat, that the worst thing that could happen would be for someone to be right there, smiling their jagged, broken-tooth smile, fingers bleeding at the quick and leaving greasy red smears.

Without realizing she was doing it, Casey was sitting on her bed looking at the undersides of her shoes, picking pebbles out of the rubber. She heard a crunching, abrasive sound. She was grinding her teeth, had swallowed her gum. No, it was on the edge of her desk in a little puddle of spit. She'd spat it out.

There was a tiny piece of gravel in her fingers. It would take just as much effort, be just as inconsequential, to toss it out into the hallway as it would to lay it on her tongue, swallow, out of sight and gone in seconds. No one the wiser either way.

Finding the body in the cabin had been a predictably traumatic experience, upsetting for everyone. The police were able to find out who she was. She had family but had been homeless for years. They guessed she'd been squatting in the cottage all winter and either got sick or starved. Never went down the street to ask for help. Casey asked if anyone had a picture of what she looked like, so she could imagine a face other than the mummified husk she'd seen, but no one would show her. Everyone refused to tell her the woman's name so she couldn't even search for her online.

There was the initial shock, of course, but after that Casey didn't really think that much about it. For the first month or so, she was concerned for her father who seemed both jumpy and zoned out at the same time. She could walk right up to him without being noticed until she touched him on the shoulder and he'd jump at least a foot. Her family was so focused on how affected he'd been that they would shut her down if she started to mention that she knew the woman had been there hiding on the last trip out to the cottage. That she'd seen someone in the window. They seemed to forget that she had found the body, too. Her father hadn't gone up there alone. But her experience just took away from his.

It started to get to her through a recurring dream. In her sleep, she would go through the whole experience over again, exactly as it had happened. Driving up to the cottage, seeing the face in the window, and then finding no one inside. But she'd have the feeling that someone was there. Right behind her. Upstairs. Inside. An eerie feeling. Then driving away, looking at that same window and seeing nothing. And then coming back up for the next visit and seeing someone through the front door, collapsed at the foot of the stairs. Her father frantically digging to find the right paving stone with the key underneath. And the same eerie feeling, but now evolved. Casey dreamed this sequence over and over, never changing. Never quite becoming a nightmare but keeping the memory of the whole ordeal at the front of her conscious mind.

While she was having this recurring dream, as weeks and months went on, she began to question all of her other memories of the cabin. Everything she remembered was now tainted, infected, by that eerie feeling. As though the woman had been hiding in the cottage all of Casey's life. She had always been there. The first night Casey had slept in the little room her father had built, the woman had been there, over the bed, hidden behind the wall, inside the stairs. Somewhere. Casey had spent many afternoons reading alone on the little couch downstairs while her parents walked along the beach or went into town. She had loved having the place all to herself. But now it wasn't all to herself. She had never been alone. She knew, consciously, that this was not true. But she couldn't shake the feeling. Now, in every one of Casey's memories of the cabin, that woman was there, creeping her way in bit by bit.

But then, bit by bit, Casey started to think about it less. Even to forget it. The dreams stopped for a time. But as she started to plan for school, for her move, to say goodbye to her therapist, that eerie feeling started to pulse again. So small at first that Casey hadn't even known that's what it was. She was excited, making good on the promise her therapist had given her years before; she was growing into a different person. These were all good things.

When the dreams came back, they didn't recur like they had before. They weren't the same anymore. They were rare, only once in a while and sometimes Casey didn't remember them all that vividly. The dreams began to change. They started as the same memory, the face in the window, the body on the floor. But the face of the woman kept changing. No longer a dried mask. The teeth still showing, but they were different. Broken. And the face began to fill in. It was Casey's face. Casey's old face. The lips drawn back in a rictus, because she was dead of course, and showing her broken and shattered teeth.

The old Casey had not been shed. She was behind the wall, slowly creeping her way back.

Casey hovered over the stool, her body barely touching it. Her finger was poised over the large red button. She was sweating, pictured a full bead of sweat building and dropping onto the machinery, frying the whole apparatus. She'd already pushed the button. She'd pushed it eighty-four times and eighty-four times she waited for the disembodied robot hand, the pointer finger of that nonentity to poke her in the back in the exact same spot. It poked her gently, of course. It was always gentle. Her conscious brain knew that the contact was soft, that it was not able to hurt her. But she couldn't help feeling as though she had developed a horrible bruise. The finger was going to poke her again but if it touched her one more time, it would go right through her.

It would push all the way through her flesh and all of her insides, her organs, her blood, her cells, all the inner parts would come spilling out.

"You need to push the button, Casey," the professor said. "If you aren't taking notes, then you have to push the button."

Casey gripped the pen hard enough to hurt her hand. She looked down at the notebook on her lap. "She can't be here, she can't be here, she can't be here." A messy, nearly illegible scrawl, torn through the pages in places. She looked around. Could anyone read over her shoulder? The space was so big. What was behind the walls? Were they like the fake walls her father had put up, a huge space between them and the outside? Letting in the breeze.

How could anyone be sure that there was not in fact another person, some creature, that was poking Casey in the back. There could be anyone hiding in the dark corners, behind the machinery. In the walls. She dared not turn around to see if it was the robot arm or something worse.

She took a deep breath, turned to a fresh page though it already had some pen marks where the paper had torn. She closed her eyes. She pushed the button. Almost instantly, she felt the poke in her back. It did not go straight through her. Nothing spilled out. It was loathsome.

She pushed the button again. Nothing. She opened her eyes. Waited. She touched her pen to the paper. She imagined the hand behind her reaching out slowly. Not the robot hand, though. This one was impossibly cold. Dirt under chewed and torn fingernails. Not just a pointing finger, the whole hand opening, moving closer, close enough to disturb the fibres of her shirt. Not touching her yet, but knowing full well that Casey knew she was there.

"What if she's here and I'm not?" Casey wrote.

The poke. Casey sobbed. She smashed the button down again. "Casey," it said in the professor's soft voice. She felt a full hand placed firmly on her back, covering the whole bruise.

"She's here, she's here!" Casey shrieked.

The first call from the university had been a couple of months before. This wasn't normally their business, to call in parents, they had said, but given Casey's history and her decline, they had been concerned. Casey's father had taken it seriously but didn't act right away. He wasn't sure what to do, to be honest. Now there was another call. There'd been an incident. Casey would not leave her dorm room and someone from the family would need to collect her.

He made the drive alone, promised to text Casey's mother if things were really as bad as they were hinting. He was still almost sure it would all be fine. The building was easy enough to find, he told the office he was there and they handed him keys, directed him to a room on an upper floor, tucked in the corner, that she had all to herself. He knocked. No answer. He used the key.

The room was destroyed. The desk upended, books and papers everywhere. There were deep scratches and what looked like bite marks on every wood surface that he could see. All of her clothes and bedding had been torn to pieces. Her down pillows were disemboweled, their insides covering everything in the room with a fine white softness.

"Casey," he whispered.

From the corner, she grabbed him by the hair, her mouth a horrible grin. Her teeth broken, the same snaggle tooth smile from when she was a little girl, but on a grown woman it was sinister. Her eyes were *not* Casey's. He did not know who this was. She pulled his head harder, pulling him close.

"Look!" she screamed, pointing his eyes to her legs. They were covered with scratches and dried blood. The down from the pillows had stuck all over her feet. "Feathers," she said.

I'm typing still. There will be no end to this. I hear the click clacking and my mouth is filled with a gummy, bitter after-taste. My jaw is sore, especially at the back, as though I've tried chewing something that simply won't break down. I found shreds of paper between my teeth. I try to send the words back to the source, to draw some nourishment for myself. They only feed the book.

They are not for me.

I hope you get more out of them. You have something in common with the book.

Maybe you'll be left a little fuller, after I am drained.

EXPERIMENTAL TRUE CRIME PUZZLES REVIEWER

Trying to Read in the Dark by Madison Greenlay
Unknown Publisher. 529 pages. $25
Reviewed by: Keith Cadieux

It's been more than twenty years since the arrest and infamous trial of Joel Navidson but still the case continues to pop into the news cycle. The disappearance of Navidson's wife Amanda and son Wesley, presumed now to have been ritualistically murdered, was international news in 1998 in no small part because of the bizarre behaviour of the now-convicted murderer. A few years ago, interest in the case was renewed when Wrongful Conviction Relief, a non-profit not unlike the Innocence Project in the United States, announced that they would be working on behalf of Navidson in order to see his conviction overturned. Citing several oversights and allegations of misconduct on the part of police, their position is that Navidson is the victim of a belated Satanic Panic hysteria. Now the whole debacle is in the spotlight again, this time brought into focus thanks to the new true crime book,

Trying to Read in the Dark, authored by Madison Greenlay, who is Amanda Navidson's sister.

I say true crime but in reality, I'm hard pressed to describe what this book actually is. Long before a review copy made its way to me, the manuscript had already gained a bizarre reputation in the book publishing industry. A monograph written by someone directly connected to the Navidson case would be big business indeed so there was plenty of interest on the publishing side.

The manuscript was received by all the major publishers at once, which is not by itself odd, but would normally be part of a concerted effort on the part of a large agency. At the time of this writing, well after publication of the book, Madison Greenlay remains unrepresented. In fact, she appears to be outright missing.

After sitting around and not being scooped up by one of the big five publishers, additional copies of the manuscript began to arrive in droves at the offices of smaller presses and flooded inboxes without any apparent way to respond to the sender, even to demand that they stop sending the thing out. Then copies began to arrive in review outlets. I've reached out to other reviewers and, sure enough, all of them have received at least one copy.

The book itself is not an ARC but certainly seems incomplete. The front and back cover are a nondescript black with no text, no title or byline. There is no copyright page or publisher information listed. Which prompted me to reach out again and after a few emails back and forth and several phone calls, I can not find any publisher that agreed to release the book. It does indeed have a barcode and stores are happy to accept money for it—at two different stores it cost me $24.95 plus tax—but no one in charge of purchasing recalls ordering the book.

I'm still not sure about calling *Trying to Read in the Dark* true crime, but it does start out that way. The opening chapters are candid, almost diary-like entries by Greenlay explaining some of the basics of her everyday life so many years after her sister's disappearance. Even this long after her sister's case has been effectively closed and settled, there are elements of the investigation that continue to trouble her. As her account progresses, Greenlay outlines her interactions with police at the time of the initial disappearance and Joel Navidson's eventual arrest, trial, and her later attempts to move on with her life. Over time she becomes so dissatisfied with the police version of events that she begins her own investigation, even managing—so she claims—to get ahold of the entire police file.

The crime itself is an odd one. For those who need a refresher:

Prior to the disappearances, Navidson was fired from his job at a university archive and released from his PhD program, facts which are verifiably true. According to Greenlay, this was a direct result of his growing obsession with proving the existence of a now-forgotten book publisher and their possession of a rumored "perfect" typeface.

Despite repeated censures and warnings from the university, Navidson continued pursuing research in this vein even though he never presented any evidence that backed up his claims. Even so, he submitted papers and gave numerous presentations on this topic, much to the university's embarrassment. His erratic behavior became too much of a liability for the university and so he was removed. Soon after that, Amanda and Wesley Navidson would disappear.

Amanda and Wesley were reported missing not by Joel Navidson but by Madison Greenlay after not having seen her sister or nephew for weeks. An exhaustive search never turned up either body of mother or son but did uncover three older bodies which have since been linked to Navidson but with only circumstantial evidence. His increasingly scary behaviour, such as wandering around the banks of the Red and Assiniboine rivers at night and the mumbling screed he unleashed when arrested, was enough to declare him guilty in the public's eye before the trial even began.

Greenlay is aware of several justice reform groups who believe Navidson to be wrongfully convicted and their various efforts to see him released. She is on board at least in the sense that she alleges the police did indeed get just about everything in the case wrong, but she vehemently believes Navidson should stay in prison. The police never did prove that anything "ritualistic" was at the heart of Amanda and Wesley Navidson's disappearances but if Greenlay's account is to be believed, Joel Navidson had fallen deep into an occult-tinged obsession.

Some of the behavior which creeped out the public does seem to be a substantial part of the police's case. Greenlay uses various police accounts to show that Navidson was seen several times underneath the Provencher bridge and along the riverbanks in other locations across the city dredging up the muck of the river bottom, furiously looking for something. Greenlay concedes that this odd behavior is an important clue but that police drew the wrong conclusions; their version of events claims this is proof Navidson had dumped the bodies and was ensuring they did not reemerge somewhere downriver. Admittedly, the fact that no bodies ever did turn up does poke a pretty big hole through that reasoning.

Greenlay is missing crucial details and particulars about Navidson's obsession but this is where the text becomes a nonsensical but strangely exhilarating mess. At the heart of her account is her regret and confession that by accepting the police's version of events that Joel was a murderer, she effectively denied the existence of other scenarios. Were Amanda and Wesley on the run, lost, somehow amnesiac or held captive?

In the last sixty pages or so, which vacillate between utterly incoherent and dreadfully upsetting, Greenlay is less concerned with Navidson's guilt but inching more to a need to understand his obsession and just what he was doing. She seems under the impression that if she understood this "perfect" typeface like he had, she would be able to solve the mystery of what happened to her sister and even bring her back.

I must admit that this book has a strange allure. Despite my criticisms, which I believe to be more generous than harsh, I simply can not shake this book out of my head. Its mere existence seems to have opened up an avenue of thought and anxiety otherwise unknown to me. I find myself simultaneously drawn to learn more and horrified at the prospect that even some of what Greenlay has written could be true.

Take this passage: "the thing in his eyes stared and stared without speaking and then, when it was able, moved bodies again and gave that same stare and then did speak, which is its true form. A sound and no shape. In and out of different minds each experience pulling it apart into billions and billions. A great formless black thing." I don't know what this means but it's in my mind now. There is a new worry in me that I can not articulate and though I know it is new, it is as though it's been there all along.

This worry is beginning to affect my dreams as well as my waking state. Because now I see Amanda Navidson almost everywhere. Most people know what she looks like, her picture having been a part of the news cycle for two decades. There's no reason to think this isn't a normal unconscious response. I've followed the case closely for years and have even contributed a few pieces to this very newspaper on the topic. It makes sense that reading this book would bring elements right to the foreground of my subconscious, and so they are in my dreams. But it's her and not. The Amanda Navidson I see is a version of her features. Parts of her face hang slack while others are pulled too tight. As though something else were wearing her. Or an image of her were projected onto something else.

It's easiest to think of it as only dreams. Sometimes I can't tell if it's Amanda or Madison Greenlay. In a real world plot twist, Joel Navidson is likely to soon be released under a not criminally responsible plea and the police have named Greenlay—who is now missing—a person of interest. But I see her on the street sometimes. I walk my dog along the river trails near St. Boniface and I have seen her knee deep in the water one second, only to look again and see nothing. I see her misshapen face peering in through my window. Amanda or Madison. Somehow both of them at once. These women I don't know but, after reading this book, it's as though they've been a part of me all along. If I can remember them, what next?

I'm scared I might start seeing the little boy, too.

STORY NOTES

I always like when these appear in short story collections so I thought maybe there are readers out there who might appreciate these. I've just been plugging away at them as the manuscript comes together so apologies if it seems like they bounce around a little. I hope you enjoy!

"Holding Hands"

This is probably the oldest story in the collection, definitely the first to be published. I think you can still see me trying to stay in the lines of proper, acceptable "literature." It still has an eerie tone but this is by far the most CanLit story I've ever written. Spencer's awkwardness is quite autobiographical though I never managed a summer girlfriend so a little bit of wish fulfillment mixed in there as well. The body in the pool idea came from a news story in the US, one of the Carolinas if I'm remembering right. The particulars are even more disturbing: a young woman took her son to a community pool; the boy went to several authorities saying that she was missing and he couldn't find her; several weeks later she was found at the bottom of the pool, her hair having gotten stuck to the drain; the condition of the water was so cloudy that she could not be seen through the murk and the pool had been open to the public without anyone finding the body.

"Donner Parties"

The basic idea for this one came to me at a burger joint. There were a bunch of TVs all showing a hot dog eating contest. As I waited for my order, I was weirdly captivated and disgusted at watching people jam hot dogs in their mouths, dipping the buns in water so that they could essentially swallow them whole, holding back retches as they approached the limits of their stomachs, while I was waiting for food. It was unintentionally grotesque. And it led me down the rabbit hole of what professional eaters do to prepare for competitions like this and that's how I learned about stretching the stomach with water by drinking whole gallons and immediately vomiting it back up. It seemed a rather painful and disgusting commitment, requiring a devotion seemingly out of place with the inherent silliness of an eating contest. But what if the contest itself were as serious, as dark, as the training? And so: an eating contest for cannibals! This story, and the others, all the words in front of you, they demand something from you, as they have demanded something even deeper from me.

234

"Signal Decay"

This story was published on its own in 2021 and is perhaps arguably not a horror story. If you've been reading the interlude essays here, I think you'll find more than enough to argue that it is horror, and I will of course always argue for it as such, though perhaps you shouldn't take my word for everything. The reason against this story as horror is essentially that it isn't very scary. Not in a visceral sense at least. It is an emotional story, though, and horror is perhaps the epitome of emotional storytelling. Grief is a terrible experience, one that is feared by many. Many traditional horror stories do indeed focus on grief. What is a ghost if not a metaphor for grief and what has been lost?

The basic plot for this story came from a true-life experience. A friend of my partner died suddenly. He was quite young, healthy, had a wife and young child, and was suddenly gone.

The sound design idea was borne from a love of the old sitcom *I Love Lucy*. It was one of my favorite shows as a kid and much of the description in the story about Desi Arnaz's laugh is pulled directly from my experience. The original story idea was creepier. Lori hearing Tim's laugh where it shouldn't be could have taken a much darker turn, but it was the grief that really pulled the story together for me and so the horror stayed muted. But the bones are there and they can be used to explore a huge range of emotional responses. Quiet horror can have a large resonance.

"The Aspiring Cult Leader's Hilarious Guide to Public Speaking"

This one's a bit of a cheat, on my part, I guess. This is a real podcast episode I found online while going down one of those endless rabbit holes. It was a video file, on a platform I'm sure YouKnow, but that I don't want to name here. The image was only the subtitles/transcript of speech, which is probably how I was able to remember it so well. I only heard it the once. It's since been deleted, of course. I've not found any kind of corroboration or anyone else who happened to hear it. Which is why I figured I could get around passing it off as a story of my own. No one really reads these notes, anyway. Except you, dear reader. Keep it under your hat.

"Diastema"

This one is hard to articulate much about. It was definitely inspired by more surreal horror like Michael Wehunt, particularly the story "Onanon" or the abstract dread in games like *Silent Hill*. The key image behind the creation of this story was the final one, of Iain completely toothless, trying to jam someone else's teeth into his bloody gums. The idea that it could be some kind of punishment seemed appropriate to the violence. And the dreamy nature of the stories means that I don't want to simply dive into the literal of what is actually going on. Indeed, I doubt that it can be articulated neatly or clearly. That's a misconception about some dreamy or abstract art—sometimes that abstraction is so integral to the piece, not even the artist can fully decode it.

"All That Cold, All That Dark"

This story came out of a particular situation. I was invited to take part in an event geared to new writers through the Winnipeg International Writers Festival. New authors were asked to share readings at the Oodena Circle, an outdoor observatory at The Forks. An important site to Indigenous history, it is a special place and a rare spot in North America where you can see a huge number of constellations. The event itself would be under the stars in a historically significant spot.

I do not have Indigenous ancestry but the story of the wendigo, witigo, windigo, has always stuck with me. It captures core elements of humanity in its wildness, its greed. I thought it important that the characters in the story do not understand the history of the place or the peoples into which they have inserted themselves, and yet they remain prey to it. The rules do not change for them. And the wendigo, though certainly a beast that exists outside of the narrator, its influence draws out something that was already there. Her hunger does not come from the wendigo but is only unleashed.

When it came time for the actual reading event, inclement weather meant we had to move it inside, but the inspiration still worked and this story is what came of it.

As I was working on this story, it came into my head that all of western civilization is a kind of wendigo, growing more and more enormous, ever gaunt and stretched too thin, never satiated. The whole world could be consumed in such a way. The story didn't quite fit into such a large scope, but it's an idea I still find interesting.

"The Accursed Share"

This is an odd one and perhaps too much of such a particular time. Though I admit the story can be a touch obvious and it may not resonate outside of a particular cultural moment, there are still some images and ideas here that I think hold interest. The wisp of hair and its possession of a body are still unsettling images. And the dark liquid throughout may make it seem as though I am not too subtly railing against big oil which wasn't the point. It was just meant to signify rot and decay, overall corruption. Something gross. This one also has more of an ironic and hopefully sometimes comical tone. Most of the stories here are deadly serious, something I am accused of being in real life, so this is also an attempt to inject just that little bit of fun into the murk.

"Lorem ipsum dolor sit amet, consectetur adipiscing elit, sed do eiusmod tempor incididunt ut labore et dolore magna aliqua. Ut enim ad minim veniam, quis nostrud exercitation ullamco laboris nisi ut aliquip ex ea commodo consequat. Duis aute irure dolor in reprehenderit in voluptate velit esse cillum dolore eu fugiat nulla pariatur. Excepteur sint occaecat cupidatat non proident, sunt in culpa qui officia deserunt mollit anim id est laborum."

"My Son, the Insomniac"

This is an idea that I've been working on since the first season of *True Detective* and I jumped on the bandwagon of many other horror writers exploring Robert W. Chambers' *The King in Yellow*. The *True Detective* version was an interesting take on the idea. The mystery surrounding the figure was so compelling and the version created by Nic Pizzolato avoided the disappointment that might come from revealing too much. What makes the King in Yellow so interesting, and so rewarding for other writers to jump in and work with, is that vagueness. That mystery. There is just enough there to really sink your teeth into but not quite enough to make concrete declarations. Every successful King in Yellow story walks this tightrope of suggestion over proof. The hint of something beyond and poorly understood. The dreamlike quality does lend it a certain Lovecraftian flavour and rather than only linking the dream to sleep, I thought the opposite could be compelling. That the complete lack of sleep could reveal just how indebted to dream we really are. It's all a dream. Or the idea that it's all a dream is a dream. It goes on forever. Where flap the tatters of the king.

"Stuck"

Am I a ghost?

Books books books.

Booky booky booky book book books. Words for the book words for the book words for the book words for the book- words fort heboo k wor sfor theb ookthebook the book the book wordsforthebookwordsforthebookswordsforthebook Lorem ipsum doret book lorem bookorem ipsbookum doret book dolor dolor book bookdolordolordouleurbook book bookbookbookbookbook teeth

This book book my book your book. This book is the book

is the book is the book. My words in the book. My books is words the words are my book. The book. It isn't mine. It doesn't belong to me anymore. It wants words. It wants my words. Words words words. Me. The book wants me. I am the book's. I belong to the book. Ipsum lorem quis nostrud exercitation ipsum lorem ipsum lorem ipsumlorenloren ipsumlomememememememememmememenotmenotme-mememememememememnotmeitsmeememememememeits-meitsitsitsitsmeiammemitsiamits

"Gizzard Stones"

An old, old idea which I struggled to find a plot that would fit. It turns out that it needed more ideas for the plot to come together. I read an article about a ghost experiment much like this, with an AI controlled mechanism that would randomly alter the interval between touching a subject. The unpredict-ability created the sensation of someone else being in the room, in control. It sort of makes me think of water torture. There too, the unpredictability of the drips is the worst part.

The pica and the bird idea just seemed to naturally go together. If a little girl were prone to eating stones, learning about other creatures that do the same would be a comfort. The presence of a version of herself dogging her, following along, trying to reemerge. I think it hits close to home for me. Especially now.

"Experimental True Crime Puzzles Reviewer"

I didn't write this one.

Photo credit – Lindsey White

KEITH CADIEUX is a Winnipeg-based writer and editor. His debut, the novella *Gaze,* was shortlisted for a Manitoba Book Award and a ReLit award. He co-edited the horror anthologies *What Draws Us Near* and *The Shadow Over Portage and Main*, which was also shortlisted for a Manitoba Book Award, as well as the 'Fantasmagoriana Series' published by the Winnipeg International Writers Festival. His short fiction has appeared in various Canadian fiction venues, including Grain, Prairie Fire, and ELQ and has been translated into French. Two short stories of his ("Stuck" and "Donner Parties") have appeared on the Honourable Mentions list of 'The Best Horror of the Year' series, edited by Ellen Datlow. He lives with his wife Lindsey and a big dog named Bear.

**OUR AT BAY PRESS
ARTISTIC COMMUNITY:**

Publisher – **Matt Joudrey**

Managing Editor – **Alana Brooker**

Substantive Editor – **Susie Moloney**

Copy Editor – **Courtney Bill**

Proof Editor – **Danni Deguire**

Graphic Designer – **Lucas c Pauls**

Layout – **Lucas c Pauls and Matt Joudrey**

Publicity and Marketing – **Sierra Peca**

Thanks for purchasing this book
and for supporting authors and artists.
As a token of gratitude, please scan the
QR code for exclusive content from this title.